DH

FRIDAY'S
STATION

FRIDAY'S STATION

•

Kent Conwell

AVALON BOOKS
NEW YORK

PRINTED IN THE UNITED STATES OF AMERICA
ON ACID-FREE PAPER
BY HADDON CRAFTSMEN, BLOOMSBURG, PENNSYLVANIA

To Ryan and Rhett, my grandsons;
and especially to Vince,
a friend who took of his time to prowl the countryside
around Tahoe to help my research;
and to Gayle—thanks for putting up with a writer.

Chapter One

WANTED
Young, skinny, wiry fellows, not over 18.
Must be expert riders.
Willing to risk death daily.
Orphans preferred.
Wages $25 a week!

The first time I spotted that ad for the Pony Express was in a saloon in Wichita, Kansas. I was an orphan, but I was ten years too old. I laughed at the poster, never figuring that down the road I'd find myself riding in tandem with the Pony Express, compliments of its founders, Messrs. William H. Russell, John Majors, and William Waddell.

But that's exactly what happened except I was a

good piece farther west at a place called Friday's Station, the Pony Express way station on the California-Utah Territory border just below Lake Tahoe.

I latched on to the job figuring on a nice, soft go-around as stationmaster for the winter. After all, two riders a day, even in the winter, was no trouble. During the spring and summer, the Holston Stagecoach came through three times a week, stopping for a short rest. Fall and winter, it circled south to avoid the snowfall.

Even during those months, the only horses we handled at the station were the Pony Express remounts—tough, iron-hard little mustangs. The stage changed teams farther west at Yank's Station.

Speaking of iron, come springtime, I had an iron-clad deal with Bo Simmons of South Texas to ramrod three thousand head of ornery beeves to market up in Kansas.

But instead of the soft go-around I anticipated, I found myself nursemaid to a new baby, two children, and a young woman from the Washoe tribe, along with a one-armed Paiute Indian boy, a patrol of soldiers with a load of Union gold bound for Abraham Lincoln, and a late-winter attack by a stirred-up passel of renegade Paiutes.

Given my choice, I'd much rather have been back in that saloon in Wichita, Kansas, laughing at the Pony Express poster and drinking good whiskey.

I never considered myself educated, not like the teachers and people in those places called colleges, but I read constantly, beginning back when I grew up in Greene County, Tennessee, where Davy Crockett grew up.

Now, I didn't kill me no bear when I was three, but I did when I was twelve, and thank heavens, I did it just before he killed me.

I shot him with a .50-caliber Kentucky long rifle, but he kept coming, which didn't surprise me too much, considering the unsociable disposition and testy temper of most grizzlies. I had two .44-caliber belt pistols. When he was just a few feet from me, I fired point blank at his thick skull, then jumped out of the way.

Or so I thought.

Right then I found out the hard way that those grizzly bears could turn on a quarter and give fifteen cents change. Except the change he gave me was two claws down the side of my face, taking off part of an ear.

I took off running, doing my dead-level best to play second cousin to a scared rabbit. I darted down a narrow trail that twisted through the forest of ancient oak and shaggy hickory. And Mr. Grizzly stayed right on my heels. I heard him grunting behind me. I ran faster, but as limber and fast and scared as I was, I still knew I couldn't outrun him.

Having hunted this part of the forest for years, I

knew every gully, hill, and tree like I knew my last name, which at that moment I couldn't remember because I was so scared. Around the next bend, there was an old hickory tree, hollowed out up to an opening fifteen feet high where a limb had broken and plunged to the ground.

I shot into the base of that hickory and shimmied up to the hole in the trunk. I pulled out my last belt pistol as the grizzly reared up on his hind legs and swatted at my head when I poked it out the hole. He ripped great chunks of hickory wood from the old tree just below the hole.

He opened his mouth wide and started growling. With blood running down my face and dripping on my arms, I shot him down the throat. He sort of froze and then crumpled to the ground.

It took me a few years to get used to folks staring at my half ear, but after a time, I forgot all about it. I was plug-ugly anyway, so half an ear more or less didn't hurt a thing. Probably added to my charm, I told myself.

But to return to my story and Friday's Station, the winter of 1860–61 in the Sierra Nevadas wasn't as fierce as some winters the old-timers remembered. They claimed a mild winter was any winter that you didn't have to climb out of the chimney to leave the house, although that seems a little far-fetched to me.

Despite the blizzard outside, me and Friday—a one-armed Paiute Indian boy who had shown up on my doorstep begging for food—were snug and warm in front of the cheery flames in the fireplace. We had sent the westbound rider out about an hour before the storm struck.

And when it roared in around noon, we hurried inside out of the weather. The way station was a single long room that served as an office, cookshack, and living quarters. Beneath one of the bunks was a trapdoor to a tunnel that came out in a windfall of tumbled pines on the banks of a creek behind the station.

Outside, the wind howled mournfully. I glanced through the window and saw the tall ponderosa pines and white fir swaying wildly in the bluster. Suddenly, the door slammed open. I jerked around, my hand leaping instinctively to the butt of my Navy Colt. My eyes bugged out like a stepped-on toad frog when I saw a man cradling a woman and two children in his arms as he urged them into the station.

An icy wind screamed through the open door, chasing the dancing fire in every direction and filling the room with swirling snow. The flames in the fireplace curved and swayed like one of those shimmy-shimmy dancers at the carnival. Ashes and sparks scattered and bounced across the rough puncheon floor.

The woman staggered and fell, and the man dropped to his knees at her side.

"The door!" I shouted to Friday.

Faster than a duck after a June bug, Friday slammed the door against the blowing snow. I hurried to the kneeling man who was gently easing the scarf from around the woman's face. "Where the blazes did you folks come from?"

The man twisted his face up at me, frost and ice thick on his eyebrows and on the porkchop whiskers that grew down to his jaw. His eyes were wide with alarm. "It's my wife. I think the baby is coming."

I stared at him. "Baby? Here? No." I shook my head. "Oh, no. Babies don't get born here." I was babbling. I didn't mind tending horses, but babies? That was for someone else.

He saw the stunned expression on my face. He gave me a reassuring grin, and in a calm voice, said, "Look, Mister. Don't worry. I know what to do. All I need from you is a bed and some clean rags and hot water." He nodded to the small boy and girl looking on. "Bub and Sis there, I delivered both. Everything's going to be just fine. My name is George Wagner, and this is my wife, Beth."

Through the pain contorting her face, Beth Wagner smiled up at me. A sheen of sweat covered her pale skin despite the cold.

Wagner nodded at the towheaded children looking on silently. "And these two rapscallions are Mary and Phillip. And now, I need a bed for her."

Dumbly, I pointed at our bunks. George quickly

but gently lifted his wife and placed her on my bunk. He glanced around. Friday and I were still staring. He nodded to the fire. "Hot water. Please. And a lantern. I need more light."

I looked at Friday who quickly swung the cast-iron pot over the fire and ran outside for snow. Within minutes, he filled the pot, and I had a pile of clean rags, at least as clean as you can find around a Pony Express way station.

While we hung a lantern and gathered birthing supplies, George Wagner told us that the blizzard had caught them just before they reached the base of Kingsbury Grade. Their team spooked and ran the wagon off the road. When the traces parted from the singletrees, the horses disappeared into the storm.

According to Wagner, he planned for them to ride out the blizzard at the wagon, but he smelled our wood smoke and gambled on reaching safety before they froze. And that's when Beth's labor pains began.

George knew his business. Thirty minutes later, a squalling baby girl blistered our ears with her cries. I grinned foolishly at her, then winked at Friday.

He winked back.

"Pretty little thing," I mumbled, staring at the tiny bundle in her mother's arms. "Pretty as a new calf."

Mrs. Wagner, perspiration shining on her ashen face, tried to laugh, but her lips and forehead grimaced in pain. She mumbled, "P-prettier than a little calf, sir."

I nodded. "Yes, ma'am. Prettier than a little calf."

George looked up at me, his eyes clouding over with an unspoken fear. He rose and turned his back to his wife. He spoke under his breath. "Where is the nearest doctor?"

Nearest doctor? I shook my head. "Forget it, Mr. Wagner. He might be over to Yank's about ten miles to the southwest, but you can't reach him today. No way."

A slender, thoughtful-looking man, he gazed down at his wife whose eyes were closed, her breathing shallow despite the squirming, hungry infant at her side. "She's bleeding. I don't know what to do. We've got to get a doctor in here. I've got to find one."

I shook my head and grabbed his shoulder. "Like I said, maybe at Yank's Station. It's a hotel and trading post. You might find the doc there if you could reach it. But you can't, Mr. Wagner. Not in this weather. You'll never make it."

He glared at me, his eyes filled with a furious determination. "I've got to. Don't you understand? She'll die if I don't get help. Can you loan me a horse?"

"Yeah. Reckon that's no problem, but—"

"Then let's go."

Chapter Two

Outside, the wind moaned around the eaves. Blowing snow and sleet rattled the heavy wooden shutters. George Wagner wrapped his greatcoat about his thin frame and tied a scarf over his bowler hat and under his chin.

I tried to stop him again, but the man wouldn't listen. He ignored my pleas. "How far did you say it was to Yank's Station?"

"Ten miles or so, but it's hopeless. The snow's piling up fast. You're a fool if you try." I laid my hand on his arm.

He jerked his arm away. He kept his voice low so as not to disturb Mrs. Wagner. "That's my wife lying there, Mister. If I have to go through the fires of Lucifer for her, I will. Now, I'd be much obliged if you'd look after my young'uns and my wife until I get back." He peered out the window through the crack in the shutters. "I guess it to be about mid-afternoon. I ought to be able to get there and back before dark."

"With the storm, it'll get dark early. And that's a heap of tough travel in this weather."

His eyes blazed with determination. "I have no choice."

I wanted to stop him, but his mind was set.

"Well, then, let's go get you a good pony. I'll try to make it to the wagon for some of your belongings. You needn't worry about your wife and youngsters. It's toasty warm here, and we got plenty of fire-wood."

He eyed me a moment, then extended his hand. "Thanks, Mister—"

"Harrison, Gabe Harrison. This here Injun boy I call Friday because I can't pronounce his Paiute name."

Wagner nodded and wrapped his scarf up over his mouth and nose, leaving only his eyes exposed.

In the barn, I saddled a tough, surefooted little mustang. "If any of these cayuses can get through, he can." I handed Wagner the reins, and he swung into the saddle. "Just give him his head. He can find Yank's Station blindfolded."

"Thanks," he said, pulling the brim of his hat down over his eyes. "Take care of my family."

I nodded, and he rode out.

I watched until he disappeared down the road toward Yank's Station. I had the sinking feeling I would never see him alive again.

Bundled in a heavy mackinaw, shotgun chaps to break the sharp wind, leather gloves, and a thick scarf, I saddled Sam, my own pony—a buckskin—and headed down the trail. Shadows were growing in the pine forest about me even though it was two or three hours until sundown. With a little luck, I could reach the wagon and put together what gear I could and then get back before the sun set.

"Come on, Sam. Dig in. We got to make some time."

I tugged my hat down on the thick scarf I had tied over my head and under my chin. I tried to draw as much of my head as possible down inside the turned-up collar of my thick mackinaw. Despite my heavy gloves, my fingers grew numb quickly.

An hour later, I spotted two horses standing hip-shot against the wind near a thick patch of antelope brush. Looking closer, I saw the harness on them and realized I'd stumbled across Wagner's team. Not far away stood the other two, staring at me.

Gathering their reins, I dallied them about the saddle horn and led the four horses on down the road until I spied the overturned wagon. The canvas top snapped and popped like a bullwhacker's whip in the heavy gusts of wind.

The wagon wasn't damaged; only the traces had broken. At first, I considered righting the wagon, but the snowfall had increased, and daylight was fading fast.

Hurriedly, I lashed as much of the belongings to the animals as possible and headed back to the way station. By now, the snow had piled several inches over the road and built drifts against the boulders and trees.

Time dragged. Because of the swirling snow, I became disoriented, losing track of exactly where I was. I reminded myself that all I had to do was continue forward and stay between the wall of pines on either side.

Despite the chilling wind and bitter snow, I felt sweat run down my sides. I couldn't afford to stop, and before long, I wouldn't be able to see my hand in front of my face.

That was when the mountain lion decided he was hungry.

I felt Sam stiffen, then sidestep. The horses behind pulled on the reins, and then I heard the yowl of the lion, almost like the scream of a frightened woman.

"Easy, Sam, easy," I muttered, leaning forward and rubbing his neck, at the same time squinting into the rapidly approaching dusk. I leaned back, withdrawing my Spencer from the boot. I jacked a shell in the chamber.

The lion howled again, this time closer. Sam hesitated, then half-reared, pawing at the air.

Off to our right, I spotted a shadow gliding across the snow. Without taking aim, I threw a shot toward the shadow.

The lion roared again. I pulled the saddlegun into my shoulder and searched the woods in front of me. Ahead, the road curved around a snow-capped ridge of granite that looked like a giant spearhead. The way station was half a mile beyond.

My pony stutter-stepped. "Whoa, Sam. Whoa, there. Easy, easy."

Sam stamped around nervously while I sat in the saddle and waited. I held the Spencer at my shoulder and kept my eyes on the crest of the granite monolith. If the lion was stalking us, that's where he would be. Waiting for us to pass under so he could drop and sink his fangs into one of the horses' necks. I decided to wait him out.

Minutes passed. Darkness began creeping through the forest in my direction. I had to move now while I could still see. With a click of my tongue and a nudge of my heels, I sent Sam forward.

I craned my neck as we passed under the granite ridge. Maybe I had been mistaken. Maybe that shot had driven the lion off. Maybe—

A guttural yowl proved me wrong. I jerked around

to see the lithe creature stretched out in the air hurtling down at one of the horses. I threw out the Spencer with one hand, aimed, and fired.

The lion screamed.

The horses broke loose and stampeded past me as the mountain lion slammed to the ground. By now, Sam had wheeled about to face the lion, and I put two more slugs in the animal. Then I hesitated, my finger tight on the trigger.

The lion lay motionless.

I muttered a curse and jerked Sam back around. "Come on, boy. Let's run them crazy broomtails down." I jammed my Spencer back in its boot as he leaped forward.

Suddenly, the flare of a torch appeared ahead.

It was Friday, and he was holding the team when I arrived. The flaming torch had been stuck in a snowbank.

"I'm glad to see you," I said as I rode up. "I didn't know if we'd make it back."

His slender face was somber. He dipped his head toward the way station. "The white woman, Gabe. She is much sick. I think she will die."

Chapter Three

I rushed inside while Friday stabled the animals and tossed them some hay. Beth Wagner lay without moving, her breath coming in almost imperceptible gasps.

The two children slept soundly on a pallet beside the fireplace. The new baby lay bundled in a box next to the bunk.

All I could do was mutter a short prayer. What in the blazes was I going to do now?

Then the baby started crying.

Mrs. Wagner opened her eyes and turned her head to her child. She struggled to sit but fell back weakly. She cradled her arm at her side and looked up at me, her eyes pleading. Gently, I lifted the infant and placed her in her mother's waiting arm.

I'm fairly dumb about women things, so when she fumbled with the buttons on her dress, I couldn't figure out what she had in mind.

Her fingers kept slipping off the hard pearl buttons. She looked back up at me and tried to speak, but no words came. Slowly, painfully, she drew her tongue over her parched lips. "Please," she whispered, touching her fingers to the buttons on her dress.

Now, it don't take a genius to spot a goat in a flock of sheep. She wanted me to unfasten the buttons so she could feed her child.

I've always been mighty uncomfortable around ladies, but right then, the most natural thing in the world for me to do was as she asked.

Perspiration rolled down her pale face as she tenderly guided her daughter's small face under the flap in her dress.

I looked away, but I could hear the baby eagerly nursing with all the enthusiasm of a new foal. I checked the sleeping children, then turned to the fire.

Friday returned at that moment. "The animals, they are good." He glanced at Mrs. Wagner.

I shrugged. "We need to get some grub down her. And I reckon the kids'll be starving when they wake up."

"We have venison in smokehouse."

"A hot stew will help. You watch them. I'll cut off some steaks if the haunch ain't frozen solid. Put some more coffee on. I don't know if our eastbound rider will make it through the storm or not, but he's due soon. I'll saddle him up a pony while I'm out there."

Friday had come to me from a nearby camp of Yosemite Indians where he had been run out of the village after losing an arm. Seems like the Yosemite only wanted healthy slaves. That was back in the early autumn of 1860, at the end of the Paiute War and just after I took over as stationmaster at Friday's Station.

I called him Friday because I was in the middle of a book by Mr. Daniel Defoe, *Robinson Crusoe*, one I had read four or five times. I figured we were pretty much like the two characters in the book— one shipwrecked, the other an outcast.

He was about thirteen or so, and he had an uncanny knack with animals, especially the green-broke mustangs we used for the Pony Express. Those ornery, hardheaded cayuses enjoyed nothing better than nipping a chunk out of your arm or busting your knee with a hoof.

Except around Friday. No matter how jittery, as soon as they spotted him, they calmed down.

In the few months we'd been together, I decided that when I left in the spring for the cattle drive from Brownsville, Texas to Wichita, Kansas, I was taking him with me. Why, he could even go on up to Wyoming with me when I bought my ranch.

* * *

In the barn, the spare *mochila* lay on the ground. I hung it back on the wall. The *mochila* was the saddlebags used by the Pony Express. It was made up of four bags fastened in such a manner that they could be thrown over the saddle and the rider could swing astride them.

Hastily, I saddled a tough little bay for the east-bound Express rider and tied him in the holding shed just outside the station. I then went into the smoke-house and pulled down an almost-frozen haunch of venison that I carried back inside where I hacked off several chunks.

Friday had the water on and was rolling out some sourdough that we dropped in the stew for dumplings. A steaming bowl of venison stew with dumplings put enough steel in a man to take him through a half-dozen blizzards.

"M—mister . . ."

I looked around.

Mrs. Wagner was looking at me through half-closed eyes. "Mister—"

"Harrison, ma'am. Gabe Harrison. Folks call me Gabe. Short for Gabriel."

She forced a smile. Her voice was weak. "Gabriel. A good name. Gabriel." She cut her eyes to the nursing infant. "My children. Pl-please take care of them until . . ." Her words drifted off. Her eyes closed.

I took a step toward her, thinking maybe she had

died, but she opened her eyes again and said, "Until George . . . comes back."

I knelt by her bunk and laid my hand on hers, which was cupped over her nursing child's head. "Don't you worry none, ma'am. Friday here and me'll take care of all of you until your husband comes back. Just don't you fret, you hear? You just rest. We'll have some hot grub that'll put you right back on your feet."

She smiled weakly, and then seemed to sag back in the bunk. The baby continued nursing.

I rose and stepped back. Should I put the child back in its box? Or let it keep eating? I'd seen foals and calves eat until they made themselves sick. I wondered if babies did the same.

Mrs. Wagner made the decision for me. Fumbling, she eased the infant's head back and nodded to me. Hands shaking, I lifted the tiny bundle.

Mrs. Wagner whispered. "Your shoulder."

I glanced at Friday who was watching intently. "Put baby on shoulder, Gabe. That's what Paiute mothers do."

I didn't argue, but placing the baby on my shoulder didn't make sense until I laid her there. Moments later, a resounding burp sounded in my ears, and I felt something hot and wet running down my back.

Friday giggled and turned back to the stew. Mrs. Wagner just smiled weakly and mumbled, "You can put her back in her bed now."

As soon as I tucked her in, I changed shirts, wrinkling my nose at the sweet smell soaking my plaid shirt. Babies and me didn't mix.

By the time I finished, Mrs. Wagner had fallen into a restless sleep, moaning and twisting.

I had no idea what was wrong with her, but whatever it was had prompted her husband to pull foot out of here at full chisel. I figured if I just kept her warm, and maybe got some food down her, she'd be all right until he made it back, if he did.

Friday filled a wooden bowl half full of steaming stew and dumplings. I knelt at Mrs. Wagner's side and touched the tip of the spoon to her lips. At first, she didn't move, and then she pulled back, turning her head.

"Please, ma'am. You need your strength." I felt something damp on my knee, but I figured it was the melted snow. "The baby, she needs you to be strong." I eased the spoon forward, but her lips remained clamped.

I glanced at Friday who was standing across the bunk. He said nothing, but I read his thoughts in his dark eyes. Outside, the wind howled about the eaves like hungry wolves, rattling the shutters and shaking the door.

"Sure wish you would take a bite, ma'am. Just one bite, and I'll stop pestering you. Please."

She had fallen asleep.

Muttering a soft curse, I rose.

"Aiyee!" Friday yelled, staring at my knee.

I looked down and saw a dark stain. Suddenly, I realized it was blood. Quickly, I peered under the bunk. A pool of blood was forming. Mrs. Wagner was bleeding to death.

Chapter Four

The Regulator clock on the mantel chimed nine. The eastbound rider was three hours late. I looked back at Mrs. Wagner. She had grown paler. I had to do something. I couldn't let her bleed to death.

Friday watched me intently.

Then I thought of the Yosemite camp back to the northeast, the one Friday had come from. I had met their chief, Ten-ie-ya, not long after the one-armed boy showed up on my doorstep.

I had paid the chief a visit because I wanted to make certain the boy was not a runaway. He assured me the tribe had driven the boy out because he was not a whole human. But, the chief added, he himself missed the boy something fierce and felt some type of recompense from me was in order.

22

After much wrangling, I paid the chief a double eagle, only to later learn that the old chief was the one who had run the boy out of camp. I reckon he saw a country bumpkin like me coming and decided to take what he could get.

"Is there a medicine man in the Yosemite camp, Friday?"

"Yes. Job-ea-toyo. He make much medicine." The bright-eyed young man pointed to his stump just below the shoulder. "He make this good. Not much blood. The Sun and Moon look on him as their son."

I reached for my mackinaw. "Listen. I'm going to get him down here. The pony is in the holding shed if the Express rider gets here before I make it back." I laid my hand on his shoulder. "You take care of things here. We got food. If the children wake up, feed them. I'll be back as soon as I can."

He nodded emphatically. "Do not worry, Gabe. Friday do good job for Mr. Willam H. Russell."

I laughed and scrubbed his hand playfully with my hand. William H. Russell was one of the founders of the Pony Express.

A few months earlier, the ponies had broken out of the corral. We chased them through the ponderosa pines and among the jagged granite until we were exhausted.

Friday looked up, sweat rolling off his cheeks and soaking his shirt. "We can not catch them."

I laughed. "We got to, son. What do you think Mr. William H. Russell pays us for?"

And find them we did.

And ever since that time, whenever Friday wanted to let me know he was going to do his very best, he promised me that he would do his all for William H. Russell.

In the barn, I saddled Sam and rode out. I left the lantern burning, a tiny light in the black night to guide me back.

The snow had ceased although clouds remained thick. I pointed Sam in the direction of the Yosemite camp, letting him make his way through the forest of ponderosa pines, tall, stately sentinels standing mute.

Despite my layers of clothes, the chilling cold crept in, numbing me to the bone. The forest of pines and fir broke the wind, so at least Sam and me didn't have the icy edge slashing at us.

I lost track of time, but soon I smelled the wood smoke from the Yosemite camp. Sam whinnied and tossed his head. I felt him change direction a few degrees. The pungent odor of wood smoke grew stronger.

Twenty minutes later, I reined up on the crest overlooking the small camp. The glow of fire diffused through the open flaps in the tops of the teepees. Dogs barked and half a dozen door flaps opened and dark figures stepped out.

I rode in slowly. Five minutes later, I reined up in front of Chief Ten-ie-ya's teepee. He stood motionless, wrapped in his thick buffalo robe. The light from his fire reflected off his face. I nodded. "Chief. I come to ask the Yosemite for help."

He grunted and turned back inside. I followed. Once inside, I removed my broad-brimmed hat and pulled off the scarf I had tied over my head and under my chin.

The Yosemite had always been hospitable to me, and in the middle of the night, they didn't forget their manners, something that can't be said about some of the more civilized cultures. The chief's wife muttered softly to three or four women lying under robes on one side of the teepee. One jumped up and brought me a hot drink, some kind of tea, and then hurried back to her robes, all the while keeping her eyes averted from mine.

I don't know what the drink was, but it quickly pushed the chill from my bones.

Fortunately, Chief Ten-ie-ya's wife had been around whites more than I had around Indians. Using my hands to form a rocking cradle, I explained, "Woman with baby. Woman bad sick."

Ten-ie-ya and his wife looked at each other. She rattled off a couple of sentences. He nodded and turned back to me. "Bad sick. Woman."

"Yeah." I pointed in the direction of the way station. "Medicine man, Job-ea-toyo, go . . . help?"

Again, he and his wife exchanged looks, and she rattled off some more Yosemite jargon. He shook his head. "Not go for squaw. Go for warrior, not squaw."

Even though I had not even considered the possibility of such an answer, his decision did not surprise me. The Yosemite, as many tribes, were patriarchal. Women were second-class citizens, although chiefs' wives and daughters were not subject to the same discrimination.

I made a face. "But she is sick, much sick. I think she might die." I closed my eyes and dropped my chin to my chest.

His wife barked a few words. When I looked up, the young woman who had brought me the tea rose to her feet and nodded submissively to the chief's wife.

Chief Ten-ie-ya smiled proudly at me and pointed to the young woman. "She Rock-in-Hand. She go. She make better."

Rock-in-Hand kept her eyes downcast.

What good was a young woman? I shook my head. "Sick. Woman is much, much sick. She lose much blood after baby."

The chief's wife and the young woman exchanged hurried glances, their eyes revealing their unspoken understanding of the problem. She spoke quickly to her husband. He nodded and turned to me. "Rock-in-Hand Washoe squaw. She make good medicine. Child die." He tapped his forefinger to his forehead. "She much good medicine. Stop blood."

I didn't understand much of anything he said, but I couldn't see any other choice. I rose quickly and thanked him. "We go now."

The lithe young woman quickly placed several items in a parfleche bag, then wrapped a thick robe about her. She looked at Ten-ie-ya who nodded once.

Outside, a small pinto stood hipshot beside Sam. The clouds had blown away, leaving a sky filled with glittering stars.

We headed back along our old trail, moving as fast as possible. Neither of us spoke. There was nothing to be said.

An hour later, we rode up to the way station. Friday ran out, his face filled with alarm. He hesitated when he saw Rock-in-Hand. I saw the surprise on his face.

"How is she?"

He shook his head. "Not good." He pointed down the road. "The Express rider has not come."

I wrapped the reins about the hitching rail and hurried inside. Almost midnight. I'd been gone three hours. The rider was six hours late. Had something happened? Maybe he had lost the trail, which was unlikely, or maybe he never made it over Echo Summit.

Beth Wagner lay motionless, her skin pasty and waxen. Her breathing was shallow and slow.

Rock-in-Hand took over. She nodded in satisfaction when she saw the pot of hot water over the fire. She reached for the blanket covering Mrs. Wagner, then hesitated. The young midwife looked at us, then waved the back of her hand at us, indicating we were either to turn around or leave.

"Let's put up the horses, Friday," I said, giving the young woman a smile.

While we were unsaddling the ponies, a drawn-out "Halloo" echoed through the night.

The eastbound Pony Express rider.

"Get him some coffee. I'll get the pony."

By the time I had the fresh remount ready, the rider was less than a quarter-mile away, a stark, black silhouette against the snow. Friday stood nearby, cupping a steaming mug of coffee liberally sprinkled with corn liquor.

Even before the exhausted pony slid to a halt, the young rider leaped from the saddle, the *mochila* in his hand. I steadied the nervous little bay as the youth swung into the saddle and reached for the coffee. He didn't look to be more than fourteen or fifteen.

He slurped the hot liquid greedily. "Sorry I'm late. Snow's bad."

"You okay, son?"

"Yes, sir."

"You run across a man named George Wagner back at Yank's?"

He sipped the coffee. "Nope."

"What about on the trail? Run across anyone?"

He shook his head. "Nary a soul. Word is, Stationmaster, a load of gold is coming through from Sacramento. Gold bound for President Lincoln's armies. A patrol of Union boys is guarding it."

I held the reins tight. An empty feeling settled in the pit of my stomach. Wagner hadn't made it. Blast the man. I'd tried to warn him, and now, he was probably lying out there under a foot of snow. No one would find him until springtime. I crossed my fingers that I was wrong.

"Keep an eye out for the wagon, Stationmaster. The gold is mighty important."

"Don't worry. We'll help them get through. You're new, aren't you?"

He downed the last of the coffee and pulled on the reins. The bay reared. "Yes, sir. Other rider got shot by hostile Paiutes. I had to take his place. Name's Cody. Bill Cody." He dug his heels into the bay. "Watch out for that gold," he yelled as he raced up Kingsbury Grade toward Daggett Pass.

I said a short prayer for him. He had to cross

Daggett Pass at night. I waved after the young man. "Take care, Bill Cody."

Within brief seconds, he had disappeared into the night. I couldn't help admiring the young man, and all the young men who had mustered the courage to take on such a daunting job.

I shook my head and stared into the darkness after the young fifteen-year-old out in the middle of the snow-swept Sierra Nevadas delivering precious words to the East.

Overhead, the stars glittered brightly. I winked at Friday. "Well, boy, let's stable and feed the pony. Then I wouldn't mind some of that coffee and a bowl of hot stew. What about you?"

He grinned. "You don't suppose Mr. William H. Russell would mind?"

I chuckled and draped my arm over his shoulder. "I don't reckon Mr. Russell would mind one bit. Not even if I added a dollop of Monongahela whiskey to my coffee."

Inside, I jerked to a halt.

Rock-in-Hand was kneeling by the bed, staring down at Beth Wagner. When we entered, the young woman raised her head and stared at me.

I read the truth in her eyes, but I didn't want to believe it. I had to hear the words. "Is-is she . . ."

A brief nod gave me my answer.

Beth Wagner was dead.

Chapter Five

W hile the children slept, we wrapped Mrs. Wagner in a clean blanket. We placed her in the smokehouse, and I put together a rough pine casket. We
then laid the casket across two sawhorses in the
smokehouse, which, besides our living quarters, was
the only building secure enough to keep out the wild
animals.

With the weather being so bitter, Mrs. Wagner
would be fine until her husband could return to give
her a proper burial.

But what if he didn't return? If he didn't, I reckoned the only thing to do was send the youngsters
to a church home in Sacramento. I didn't envy the
children such a fate. I'd lived through foster homes,
and I wouldn't wish them on anyone.

As I closed the smokehouse door on the casket, I suddenly remembered the new baby. Babies need milk. Where in the blazes was I going to find milk for the child?

Maybe the Yosemite had some goats. But even if they did, I reminded myself, none of them would be fresh this time of year.

The only other option, Sacramento, was over a hundred miles away.

To the east, the sky began growing lighter.

Shaking my head in the mess I'd suddenly found myself in, I returned to the station, seriously considering a weeklong drunk. I knew I wouldn't but it didn't hurt none to consider the idea.

I stomped inside and brushed the snow from my mackinaw and chaps. To my surprise, Rock-in-Hand sat by the fireplace, a blanket modestly draped over her shoulders while she nursed the infant. Then I understood what Chief Ten-ie-ya had meant when he remarked "child die." Rock-in-Hand's own child had died.

Mary and Phillip looked up from the sawbuck table where they were eating bowls of hot stew. The girl looked past me, searching for her mother. I figured she was about six, the boy maybe four. Neither spoke, but I could tell from the puzzled expressions on their faces that they couldn't quite figure out where their mother and father had gone.

I was no good with kids, but I figured they were about like grownups and wanted to have things explained to them. So I did, sort of.

"Look, youngsters. Your pa has gone for help. Him and your ma will be back later. They want you to wait here for them. Understand?"

Phillip stared at me, then looked up at his sister. Mary nodded, then elbowed her little brother. "Eat, Phillip. Mommy wants us to eat and be nice. They haven't forgotten us."

I glanced at the clock on the mantel. Almost seven.

When the Express riders were on schedule, we had a westbound in around ten o'clock each morning and eastbound at six o'clock each afternoon except Sundays.

Winter snows played old Ned with our schedules, but thanks to those gritty mustangs and hardheaded riders, we were never more than six or so hours late.

Bill Cody had come through only a few hours earlier heading east. We should be getting a westbound in the next few hours depending on the drifts at Daggett Pass at the top of Kingsbury Grade.

I reckoned I had time to put myself around a couple of bowls of Friday's venison stew and down a few cups of six-shooter coffee.

While I was poking grub down my gullet, Rock-in-Hand placed the baby on her shoulder, patted her a few times on the back, and was rewarded with a hearty little belch. Unlike my experience, the baby didn't christen her with a mouthful of secondhand milk.

I studied the young Washoe woman as she placed the infant in its box and hummed softly to the child. Her braided hair, so black it appeared almost blue, hung over her shoulder as she stared down at the child. When the baby had fallen asleep, Rock-in-Hand turned back to the fireplace. She moved noise-lessly across the floor, almost gliding. Without a glance to either side, she filled a bowl with stew and squatted cross-legged in front of the fire.

I caught Friday's eye. "Doesn't she want to sit at the table?"

He spoke to her in the vernacular of the Yosemite. She glanced at me, then replied.

The young boy grinned. "She says she is a squaw. Squaws, especially slaves, do not sit with the men."

I chuckled. "Well, you tell her that she ain't no slave here. I'm grateful for her help, and I'd like for her to sit at the table with you and me and these kids."

His dark eyes danced with merriment. He jab-bered off a string of words. She cut her eyes at me. A flicker of a smile touched her lips and then van-ished so suddenly that I wasn't sure I had even seen one.

Without a word, she rose and came to the table,

her moccasined feet silent as a spider on its web. She sat beside Mary.

The little girl smiled up at her. "My name is Mary. He's Phillip. He's my brother. What is your name?"

The young Washoe woman laid her slender hand to her chest. Her face remained impassive as she replied, "I am called Rock-in-Hand."

I looked at her in surprise. She knew our language.

Mary giggled. "That's a funny name."

Rock-in-Hand's eyes glittered with amusement, but her face remained somber. "Mary is funny name."

Both children giggled.

I cleared my throat. "How is it you were with the Yosemite?"

She shrugged. "I was taken prisoner by Apache when they attack my people. They sell me to the Yosemite." She paused, thinking. "It was the Year of the Dead Harvest."

Friday broke in. "That was the year of my birth. I hear old men talk of that year. Many tribes had little to eat."

Suddenly, Phillip started crying and calling for his mother. I just stared at him. What do you do with a squalling child? I looked at Friday who simply shrugged.

Rock-in-Hand took over. She slipped down by

Phillip's side and cradled the boy to her. She made soft, soothing sounds.

The boy buried his head against her chest. His cries subsided. "Indian children do not cry," she said in a whisper, caressing his sandy hair. "You do not cry. Your mother would not want it."

Phillip snuffled once or twice and gave her a weak grin.

She glanced at Mary. Rising, she led the children to the blanket where she retrieved a hairbrush from Beth Wagner's valise and began brushing Mary's hair.

Leaving Rock-in-Hand and the children, Friday and I went out in the crisp, clear morning to saddle the pony for the Express rider. We tended the other animals, breaking the film of ice over their water and making sure they had an ample supply of hay.

Outside, Friday nodded to the clear sky and grinned at me, his white teeth a sharp contrast to his dark skin. "Maybe the snow will melt some." He led the saddled pony to the shed in front of the station and tied him in the stall to await the west-bound rider.

"Maybe," I replied, grabbing the bow saw off its nail and closing the barn door. I nodded to the wood rack. "But we got to cut us some more firewood while the weather holds. You hear?"

I preferred California black oak firewood because

it burned cleaner, but in this part of the country, most of our firewood came from the ponderosa and lodgepole pine, which was responsible for burning many a building to the ground when the excess of resin inside the fireplace caught fire.

We had a stack of forty or fifty ten-inch diameter pines that we worked on. We started at one end of the stack cutting off two-foot lengths from each log.

From what I had been told just after hiring on in the autumn, fifty pines would get us through the winter. I hoped so. I wasn't anxious to find myself forced to cut down more pines and haul them in.

I cut, and Friday hauled.

Suddenly, a distant shout caught my attention. Standing near the top of the stack, I peered to the east, toward Daggett Pass.

A dark figure on horseback came lurching through the snow. "Grab some coffee, Friday. Here he comes."

The appearance of the Pony Express rider galvanized us into action. Leaving the saw in the log, I hurried to the holding shed. Itching to get under way, the black mustang snorted and stamped his feet as I led him out.

One of the traits I most admired in mustangs was their restlessness. In the wild, they were always on the run. Ours were green broke, which is only about half a hoot and holler from being full-blooded wild.

Friday hurried from the station with a pot of coffee in his hand and a cup tucked in his coat. He sat them on the bench beside the shed and rushed back in to fetch a bowl of his stew. Most riders could make the change of mail and horses in seconds. Give them another minute, and they could gulp down a cup of coffee and bowl of stew.

As the rider drew near, I recognized Jimmy Moore, a young, happy-go-lucky daredevil who was just as accurate with his Colt .36 as the Spencer carbine he carried on his back. A born horseman, Jimmy stuck to the saddle tighter than two coats of paint.

He slid his pony to a halt and leaped from the saddle, *mochila* in hand. He slapped the Mexican saddlebags over the saddle of the black and grabbed the coffee.

"Howdy, boy," I said. "You pass Cody?"

Jimmy nodded briefly. "Yep. Other side of Genoa. What's the trail like ahead?"

"No snow since Cody came through. Shouldn't be any problem. Keep a watch for a wagon with Union soldiers on the trail. I'm expecting them any time."

Jimmy looked up from the bowl of venison stew. "You ain't got long to wait, Gabe. Here they come." With that, he tossed the cup and bowl to Friday, swung into the saddle, and with a wild shout, dug his heels into the mustang.

He waved at the soldiers as he passed.

They waved back.

Minutes later, the wagon with its driver and four outriders, all Union soldiers, pulled up in front of the station. Right off, I noticed their saddles. Instead of the single-rigged McClellans with their toe-fendered stirrups, they rode Hope saddles, double-cinched western saddles with a Texas skirt and open stirrups. The wagon was a converted ambulance with a flat canvas top.

"Howdy," I said, waving as I strode out to greet them. "You boys light and come inside. Friday here will tend your horses." I laid my hand on the rump of one of the sorrels pulling the wagon and grinned up at the driver. I noticed a Richmond musket at his side. I'd seen plenty of them back in Kentucky and Tennessee. No one could miss the distinctive hump-back lock plate and brass butt plate.

I glanced back at the saddles, then back at the musket with a frown, curious as to what the Union boys were doing with Johnny Reb equipment.

The driver, a private, hesitated. He glanced at the sergeant, a bull of a man with shoulders wide as a singletree.

"Stay with the wagon, Private," said the sergeant. He nodded to me, flashing a warm smile. "I'm Sergeant Paul Darcy, U.S. Army. You don't mind, Stationmaster, we need a spot to rest a spell. The back wheel on the wagon is squealing something fierce. We got us some work to do on it before goin' on."

"Make yourself at home, Sergeant. Got some tools in the barn. Reckon you all know what you need."

Chapter Six

The Union soldiers tended their animals well, each brushing his remount, then feeding and watering before he looked to his own needs.

I could tell immediately that those old boys had grown up with saddle ponies. On the other hand, I was surprised, for most of the Union soldiers I had run across had grown up on farms with plow horses that were never groomed or pampered. The old plugs were unharnessed and turned into the corral and hay tossed on the ground.

Something about those old boys nagged at me. If I didn't know better, I'd figure these jaspers for Southerners.

What little I had seen up North, saddle ponies were for the gentry, and not many of the gentry found themselves serving as enlisted men in the militia or Union army. Now, if those fellers had been from Texas, I could have understood.

I shrugged. I wanted to question them about George Wagner, but I figured that could wait until later.

The driver, a beardless young man who didn't look more than seventeen or so, remained with the wagon when the others headed for the station. Sergeant Darcy hesitated when he stepped inside and spied Rock-in-Hand tending the infant. His men stepped around us and crossed the room to the fireplace.

"Come on in, Sergeant. This is Rock-in-Hand. She's Washoe, a Yosemite captive, but she's helping with the baby. This here is Friday, and those two youngsters are Mary and Phillip, the baby's brother and sister."

Darcy's eyes narrowed. He removed his campaign hat and glanced around. "Where's their mama?"

I grimaced at him and cut my eyes in the direction of the children who were staring at him curiously. "She's with their daddy. He went over to Yank's Station. Don't reckon you spotted him." I then added loud enough for the children to hear, "Their ma will be back soon."

The heavily muscled man sensed my poor lie. He studied the children, then nodded for me to follow as he stomped over to the fireplace.

His men stepped aside as he approached. I couldn't put my finger on it, but I had the feeling they were jumpy about something, just what I couldn't fathom. I reminded myself that anyone carrying gold in this part of the country had reason to be spooky. And if I knew about the gold they carried, then probably all of California and half of Utah Territory knew.

Darcy spoke in a whisper, "You say their pa went to Yank's Station?"

"Yep. Yesterday. During the middle of the storm. I tried to stop him, but his wife was sick." I glanced around at the children who were busy playing on a blanket Rock-in-Hand had spread on the floor. "Their ma died last night. We're waiting for their pa."

Darcy grunted. He looked at the corporal who nodded briefly. Darcy's eyes cut toward the children, then back to me. He looked concerned. "We found a gent froze to death about five miles to the west. Skinny, wearing a greatcoat and one of them Eastern-type hats with a scarf tied under his chin."

I muttered a soft curse. "That sounds like him. Blast." I touched my finger to my jaw. "Had pork-chop whiskers down to here?"

Darcy looked around. "Afraid so. What did you do with their ma?"

"Out back in the smokehouse. I built a casket for her. She'll be fine there until the thaw."

Friday dropped an empty coffee cup that clattered to the floor. One of the young privates grabbed for his sidearm, then hesitated.

He and Darcy exchanged a hasty look. The sergeant laughed. "Reckon we're a bit spooked what with the weather and all."

I gestured to the table. "You men sit. Grub's coming."

Mary and Phillip, startled by the commotion, sidled over to Rock-in-Hand, their wide eyes fixed on the newcomers.

Meanwhile, Friday placed bowls and cups on the table and pulled a steaming pot of coffee from the coals. "You and your men help yourselves, Sergeant. We got plenty," I said.

He nodded. "Much obliged, Mister . . ."

I extended my hand. "Harrison. Gabe Harrison."

"I'm Paul Darcy. This here is Corporal J. D. Andrews, Private Joe Henry, and Private Melvin Cook. Private Stanley Boles is out in the barn with the wagon."

The two privates nodded and grinned shyly. Corporal Andrews, a lanky man with lidded eyes, stroked his drooping mustache and grunted. He studied the interior of the station.

"Well, boys," I said, "you all help yourself."

I noticed they kept glancing at Friday and Rock-in-Hand while they forked grub down their gullets, so I explained how the two came about to be here at the station. "And then, come spring, I'm heading back to Texas where I got me a cattle drive to Wichita. Try to get enough greenbacks for a nice little spread up in Wyoming."

"You get many of them Pony Express boys through here each day?" Corporal Andrews asked as he smoothed his mustache. I had taken an immediate dislike to the man, yet I had no idea why.

"A couple." I was beginning to grow suspicious.

"When's the next due?"

"About six or so this afternoon. Hard to say for sure, Corporal."

"Oh?" He seemed to tense up. "Why's that?"

I grinned. "You seen it for yourself. The weather. Yesterday, the eastbound was six hours late. You passed the westbound when you came in. Jimmy Moore. He was about on schedule."

Andrews seemed to relax.

Darcy pulled out a bag of Bull Durham. "Fine vittles, Gabe. Mighty fine."

Private Cook chimed in, "Best grub I had since I left home back in—"

"Private!" Darcy snapped at the young man. Then his voice grew amiable. "Why don't you relieve Boles. I reckon he's hungry."

The young man shot me a hasty, frightened look, then rose. "Yes, Sergeant." He gulped the rest of his coffee and hurried outside.

Darcy smiled at me. "Melvin there is sure a talker.

Why, he's always bragging on the table his ma sets up in New Hampshire. Ain't that so, Corporal?"

Andrews stared at me with cold, unfeeling eyes. "Yeah. I reckon that's so."

I grinned and sipped my coffee, at the same time trying to figure out just what was going on. For one thing, they didn't talk like any of the Northern boys I'd been around. But on the other hand, the honest fact was that I hadn't been around that many Northern boys, so I couldn't say how they all talked.

I drained my coffee and reached for my coat. "Well, like I said, if you men need some tools for your wagon, you'll find some in the barn. Now, Friday and me got to get some firewood cut."

Bundled against the cold, Friday and I took on the stack of logs again, me sawing off length after length and Friday stacking them along the side of the station.

The Union boys spent the rest of the afternoon working on the wagon. I noticed that every time I looked up, one or the other was watching us.

The sky remained clear. That was the good news. The bad news was that clearing skies meant plummeting temperatures.

I removed my mackinaw and straightened my Colt on my hip. I was sweating despite the nippy weather.

Around five, Friday and me headed for the barn. Andrews spotted us and whispered to the sergeant, who rose to meet us. He made no effort to stop us, yet I had the feeling that was his intention.

One of the privates was working on the axle while the other two were greasing up the wheel hub. Andrews watched us warily.

I pointed to the barn. "Rider due soon. We're getting his pony ready."

Darcy's eyes played over the Navy Colt on my hip. He followed us inside and rested his arms on the top rail of the stall as we pulled out a pony. "Looks like a fine string of horses you got there, Gabe."

We saddled up a lineback dun, a mild-mannered but courageous little animal. "Yeah. Mr. Russell bought the best."

He changed the subject abruptly. "You hear about us?"

I glanced over my shoulder and grinned. "Reckon everybody's heard about you. Truth of the matter is, Sergeant, I'm surprised you don't have more men with you."

He chuckled. "I always said, you want the truth, ask somebody from Texas."

I checked the bridle, adjusting it for a snug fit on the dun. "Reckon that could be true anyplace, not just Texas."

Darcy leaned back against a stall rail. "Suppose you're right. Heard any news about all the trouble back East?"

"You mean war talk?"

"Yeah."

"Just the usual grumbling about the secession business." I led the dun from the stall. "Truth is, I can't rightly figure just what is going on. But I'm keeping my nose out of it. I just want to get through the next couple of months and then back to Texas."

He studied me warily. I had the feeling he didn't believe me. Suddenly, all those little nagging pieces about the soldiers that didn't fit started falling into place. Not all at once, but enough to make me wonder about the patrol.

Outside, I left Darcy at the wagon while I tied the dun in the holding shed to await the eastbound rider. Staring over the saddle at the boys in blue, I thought back over the afternoon. They rode in on western saddles, not Army issue. Maybe just coincidence, but they looked after their ponies the way boys in the South did, with a special care and gentleness. Of course, I reckoned that probably fellers up North did the same.

But why would Darcy ask about the war talk?

Sure, I supposed everyone had heard about the mass meeting in favor of the Union held in San Francisco last month on Washington's birthday. That just about assured that if a war came, California was against slavery.

I didn't cotton to one man owning another, but back in Texas, there were some who did, not many, but some. And there was no question in my mind that if push came to shove, Texas would fight for slavery. I disagreed right strong with that, the same way old Sam Houston did.

In a way, I sort of felt guilty because I was a Texan. No jasper likes to go against his home state.

The soldiers stood with their heads together, from time to time giving me a glance. I had the uncomfortable feeling that if I knew what they were saying, I wouldn't like it.

A halloo drifted through the pines from the west. A dark spot appeared against the snow. If there had been no problems, the rider should be Johnny Fry.

Friday hurried from the station with the coffee. I pulled out the dun and waited. The soldiers looked on with interest.

Johnny Fry leaped from the saddle and slung the *mochila* on the dun. He sipped the coffee and made a face. "What's wrong with you, Gabe? You forgot the whiskey." He laughed and tossed me the cup. He nodded to the soldiers as he swung into the saddle and turned to me. "That the gold?"

"Yep."

The dun reared. "Well, tell them to keep an eye out. I heard there's a Confederate patrol in the state somewhere looking for the gold."

His words hit me between the eyes.

"By the way," he added, "your place right here is about to become Nevada Territory. Word is last

week, Nevada broke away from Utah." He clicked
his tongue and popped his hat against the dun's
haunches. "Things is changing mighty fast in this
modern world."

Before I could reply, he was heading east, the
dun's blurred feet throwing up a spray of snow.

I glanced at Friday. Johnny Fry's words had not
made an impression on him, but they had on me.

I suddenly realized what had been bothering me.
It's hard to disguise a wolf in a herd of sheep, and
old habits are hard to break.

Could it be? Could those five be the Confederate
volunteers? Word was President-elect Abraham Lincoln wanted the gold for the Union. But what if a
band of Southern boys decided the South needed the
gold worse than the North?

Laughter burst from the group. Private Boles
clapped Cook on the back, and they laughed again.
Darcy and Andrews joined in.

I studied them a moment. Was I letting my imag-
ination run away with me? They could be exactly
what they appeared, Union soldiers following orders.

Instead of wasting time worrying about honest
soldiers doing their duty, I should be figuring out
just what to do with the children. Come morning,
I'd head down the trail to Wagner's body. If it was
him, I'd send word to Yank's by the next rider, and
let someone else decide about the children.

Still . . . I decided to pass Johnny Fry's warning

about the Confederate patrol to Darcy. See how he reacted.

Darcy arched an eyebrow, then calmly replied, "Much obliged, Gabe. We'd heard them Johnny Rebs might be trying something."

That's when I would have bet the farm they were Confederates. I just needed some proof.

Chapter Seven

Night came early during winter in the High Sierras, but the bright moon lit the snow like day. The towering ponderosa pines cut vertical slashes of black across the white countryside. In the distance, a wolf howled. The cry drifted through the pines mournfully.

I headed for the barn while Friday busied about the fireplace, frying up a platter of venison steak and baking a couple of loaves of sourdough bread. I'd taught him to make red-eye gravy, so now he prepared gravy with whatever meal we were having. Once he even whipped up a batch with some "Pecos strawberries," but I explained that red-eye gravy just isn't too tasty of a side dish with beans.

* * *

Huddled in his greatcoat with his hands jammed in the pockets and stomping his feet for warmth, Private Melvin Cook stood guard just inside the barn in a patch of lantern light. The frigid air had tinged his cheeks with red. He nodded when I entered. "Howdy, Mr. Harrison."

I nodded back. "Just Gabe, son. Just Gabe."

A grin spread over his slender face. "Okay, Gabe. I'm Mel. Short for Melvin."

I reached for the pitchfork that hung next to the axe and bow saw on the wall. A couple of bedrolls had been spread on the hay. I speared some hay from the far side of the stack and forked it to the horses. "You been in the Army long, Mel?" I was just making conversation.

"About a year, I reckon."

I chuckled. "Well, you fellers got a mighty responsible job getting this wagon to Washington."

He frowned. "What do you know about the wagon?"

"Don't worry, son. Darcy asked me if I knew about you old boys. I told him everyone did. You boys are news."

"Oh."

"You're a long way from home. I'm not certain, but isn't New Hampshire up somewhere around New York? That's a good piece from here."

He frowned. "New Hampshire?" He hesitated,

suddenly wary. "Oh, yeah. Yeah. New York. A good piece."

I cracked the ice on the water trough and fished out the larger chunks. "The others from up around your neck of the woods?"

"Huh? Yeah. Yeah, they're from up there too." He nodded and grew silent.

His sudden silence puzzled me. I finished feeding the horses, then checked saddles and bridles. When I finished, I glanced at him. "Well, I reckon that's it. Grub'll be ready in a few minutes. Reckon Darcy'll send relief out." I leaned the pitchfork against the wall next to the spread bedrolls. Then I froze in my tracks.

There was the proof I needed.

Sticking from under a bedroll was the hilt of a sword with a brass grip, pommel, and knuckle guard. In front of the knuckle guard was a clamshell guard with CSA cast into it. CSA. Confederate States of America!

I looked away, deliberately straightening the pitchfork on its nail. "I don't know about you, but I'm hungry enough eat an ox." Without looking back, I headed for the door.

As I left the barn, I met Sergeant Darcy. He nodded, his eyes searching my face.

I grinned at him. "Starting to get cold, Sergeant. A warm fire will feel mighty good tonight. Shame your men have to keep watch over the wagon."

A faint smile played over his face. "The life of a soldier, Gabe."

I laughed and continued to the station, trying to sort the thoughts tumbling through my head. This had to be the Confederate patrol Johnny Fry had mentioned. No question of it. Somehow, they had stolen the gold.

The pieces fell into place. The Texas saddles, the Richmond musket at Private Boles's side, the care they gave their animals. If the truth were known, I told myself, Melvin Cook was probably from Georgia instead of New Hampshire.

My next thought was to get word to the authorities. I paused on the porch and stared up at the moon. On the other hand, why get involved? I'd already told Darcy all I wanted was to get to that cattle drive next spring.

In Wichita, I planned on taking my wages and putting a down payment on a little spread up in Wyoming. I didn't care about all the bickering between the North and South. If they wanted to fight, just leave me out of it.

But I wondered. I was a Texan. How could I not fight for my own state? Yet, I wasn't really sure if Texas was right. I'd heard folks discuss a state's right to secede, but I couldn't really decide just how I felt about a state leaving the Union. Or *if* a state could leave. To me, that was like a son trying to leave his family. Even if he wanted to, he couldn't, for whether he liked it or not, he was always a part of the family.

But there was no war yet. There might not even be one. The plain fact was these five were nothing more than common thieves. That was something I couldn't ignore, not in good conscience.

I shook my head and reached for the front door. Seemed like folks were always starting up trouble in unlikely places causing problems for unlikely folks. Especially me.

The rest of the patrol was sitting at the table, putting themselves around piles of steak and gravy. They looked up and nodded when I entered, then returned to their repast.

The baby slept peacefully, and the two children played on the spread blanket with a couple of rag dolls Rock-in-Hand had fashioned from scraps of cloth. I looked at her and pointed to my mouth, then the platters of steaming meat. "You eat?"

She nodded. "Plenty. Friday, he make good grub."

I laughed and reached for a tin plate. I filled it with steak and hot bread, then smothered both with hot gravy from which steam rose. A boiling cup of six-shooter coffee topped off the meal.

Private Boles grinned at me when I plopped down at the table. "How cold you reckon it'll get tonight, Gabe?"

Private Henry hugged himself and shivered. "It never got this cold back home."

Corporal Andrews shot Henry a hard glance. The young man hastily added, "I mean it never seemed this cold. This is a different kind of cold than what we got up in New Hampshire."

I tried to remain casual. The last thing I needed was for them to realize I knew their identity. I could make my move after they left. "Not bad. Maybe twenty degrees or so. I'm not all that familiar with cold weather, so any of it seems cold to me."

Usually, I can put away a heaping pile of grub with gusto. Fried steak, hot bread, and red-eye gravy made up my favorite meal, but tonight, they had no taste. And I knew why. The taste of thievery was in my mouth.

I had to act natural. Otherwise, they might become suspicious.

I lowered my voice so the children wouldn't hear. "Sergeant Darcy mentioned the frozen body you boys found." I nodded to the children. "Tomorrow, I need to get up there and make sure it's their daddy. If it is, I got to do something with the children. Find family or something."

While I was speaking, Darcy entered the station and went to stand in front of the fire, warming his hands. He rolled his broad shoulders. Keeping his eyes on the fire, he spoke in an easy, conversational tone. "Afraid that won't be possible, Gabe."

I looked up in surprise, and concern.

The men at the table frowned at Darcy, puzzled. His tone didn't match his words.

He turned to face me. His arms hung loosely at his side, and I saw that he had unsnapped his holster flap. His jaw hardened. Still in a genial tone, he continued, "Let's forget the balderdash, Gabe. Straight to the grist and gristle. You know who we are, don't you?"

A chill swept over me. He knew. Somehow he realized I had learned the truth.

I'd never developed a knack for skillful lying—a regrettable neglect, which at that moment I considered one of the most critical defects in my flawed life. But I gave it a try. "Reckon I do, Sergeant, though I don't figure what's on your mind. You old boys are the Union patrol taking a wagonload of gold to Washington, D.C." I deliberately sipped at my coffee, trying to appear dumb as a snake.

Behind him, Friday stirred the coals in the fireplace, unaware of the tension growing in the room.

Darcy narrowed his eyes and gave me an amused smile. "I don't reckon I'd ever like to get in a game of stud poker with you, Gabe. I got a feeling I couldn't beat you at poker any more than I could sneak up on a sleeping weasel."

I grinned back and sat my cup on the table with my left hand. At the same time, I dropped my right into my lap. If push came to shove, I'd take Darcy first, then Andrews. The young soldiers would be too surprised to react. "That's mighty flattering, Sergeant, but you're way over my head. I don't know what you're talking about."

His eyes missed nothing. Keeping them focused on me, he drawled to his men, "Old Gabe here has us pegged, boys. He spotted that blasted saber of yours, Andrews. I told you to leave it behind."

Three sets of eyes turned as one and stared at me.

I heard a whisper behind me. I looked around to see Rock-in-Hand gathering Mary and Phillip to her. She stared at Darcy in alarm.

He continued, "You done put us between the rock and the hard place, Gabe. With riders coming through every day, you'd have word about us all over the country in a matter of days. And you know we can't have that. The gold means too much to our cause."

Corporal Andrews grunted. "Only one way we can be sure about them," he muttered, laying his hand on the butt of his sidearm.

Private Henry and Private Boles glanced at each other nervously. Boles gulped. "You . . . you don't mean to kill him. That ain't what you mean, is it?"

Andrews sneered. "You got a better idea? That gold will buy enough arms and powder for a dozen armies, enough to push them Yankees all the way back to Nova Scotia. What do you figure is best,

Private, helping our boys whip up on the Yankees or one solitary man?"

I studied Andrews and Darcy. I was fast. Always had been. Had I been alone, I would have chanced it, but I couldn't risk Rock-in-Hand or one of the children picking up a wild slug. No. Any play I made with them in the room was a fool's play.

So I did what anyone would do. I bluffed. "You said it yourself, Corporal. Riders come through every day. Something happens here, they'll know. What are you going to do, kill every rider? As soon as they stop showing up at their scheduled stations, people will get mighty curious."

Darcy grinned, grudgingly. "Well, Gabe. We got us a little predicament here. I don't reckon you would offer to keep your mouth shut, would you?"

I studied him a moment, then shifted my gaze to the others.

Before I could answer, a chilling scream came from the barn followed by several gunshots.

For a moment, we froze, staring at each other in shocked disbelief.

As one, we exploded for the door. Private Boles reached it first and slung it open. A three-foot arrow slammed into his chest, knocking him backward. Three more arrows whizzed through the open door, thumping into the far wall.

Chapter Eight

I grabbed my Colt as Corporal J. D. Andrews kicked the door shut. I pressed up against the wall and peered around the window jamb, but the reflection of the lantern on the dark glass threw a glare over the window.

"The lantern," I whispered to Rock-in-Hand. "Turn off the lantern."

She nodded and quickly did as I said, plunging the room into darkness except for the flames leaping in the fireplace. I ducked under the window and put the fire to my back so the glare would not affect my vision. From the corner of my eye, I saw Rock-in-Hand crawl to Private Boles.

Darcy growled. "What the Sam Hill is going on? Who's out there?" He glared at me, then glanced at the young man sprawled on the floor. He watched the young Washoe woman extract the arrow. "Who did this, Gabe?"

The moon reflected off the snow, painting the countryside in black-and-white relief. I squinted in an effort to discern any movement outside. Suddenly, a dark figure darted from the barn to the holding shed in front of the station.

At the same time, a plume of orange punched a hole in the night, and a window shattered at the far end of the station.

I ducked. "Beats me. The Yosemite aren't stirred up about anything. My guess is the Paiutes. They got pushed around by the Army last summer." I gestured to the windows. "Best close the shutters and bar them. Use the gun ports."

"Paiutes? I didn't know they were on the warpath."

Private Henry spoke up, his voice thin and frail. "I ain't never even heard of Paiutes. What kinda Injun are they?"

A drawn-out moan from Private Boles interrupted us. Rock-in-Hand was packing clean rags in the hole in his chest.

A barrage of gunfire from outside slammed into the station. I crouched beneath the window, listening to the sound of breaking glass. The children were huddled in a corner where Rock-in-Hand had placed them.

I was mighty grateful for the solid log walls protecting us. The only way any attacker could get to us was by burning us out, and that would take a heap of time.

As if the Paiutes had read my mind, a burning arrow crashed through a window, striking a bunk. Before the fire could get started, Rock-in-Hand yanked the arrow loose and stamped it out on the puncheon floor.

I yelled at Private Henry, "I said close those shutters!"

Peering through the gun port shaped like a cross, I searched the darkness beyond. A shadow moved, and a spurt of flame leaped toward me. Quickly, I fired. A muffled scream echoed through the night.

For a few minutes, the firing was sporadic. Without warning, a sustained volley of rifle fire slammed against the cabin.

We returned fire, aiming at the patches of yellow and orange lighting the darkness. Friday sat at my feet, reloading my Navy Colt while I steadily fired my Spencer carbine.

Darcy lowered his handgun and cursed. "You got any rifles? Ours are in the barn."

I coughed against the gunsmoke filling the station. My ears echoed with the thunder of booming rifles and handguns. "In the rack above the desk. Some Spencers and a Sharps. Plenty of cartridges."

The Johnny Rebs grabbed Spencers, repeating rifles holding a tubular magazine of seven rimfire cartridges. Each snatched up a handful of loaded magazines.

We laid down a withering barrage of gunfire. With the four of us throwing lead plums at the marauding Indians, we quickly drove them back.

Suddenly, all was quiet outside. Nothing moved. Inside, the flames cast eerie black shadows across the room.

We exchanged puzzled looks.

I muttered, "What about your gold?"

Darcy's face was grim. "We got it hid in barrels of flour. They'd have to bust it open to find it."

In the corner, the baby whimpered. Rock-in-Hand hurried to the child. I knelt by Private Boles. His breathing was short and jerky. I grimaced. The boy was lung shot. He didn't have a chance.

From the shadows at the end of the room, Private Henry whispered, "You see anything out there?"

"Nothing's moving," Andrews replied.

Darcy broke in. "Keep quiet, boys, and keep watching. How's Boles?"

The shadows played over the unconscious boy's face, giving it the appearance of a cadaver. I laid my hand over his heart that beat faintly, but steadily. "He's still breathing."

Private Henry interrupted, "Look! Behind the barn. Where are they going?"

We squinted from the windows, straining our eyes

to make out the shadows among the pines beyond the barn.

Darcy mumbled, "What do you think they're up to now?"

"I don't trust them," Andrews replied. "They might be trying to draw us out."

I strained to make out the objects. "I can't tell what they are. It could just be the wind blowing the sagebush or antelope brush."

Andrews snorted. "Not likely."

Private Henry whispered from the darkness at the end of the room. "What do you think happened to Mel? You think they killed him?"

In a hard, unfeeling voice, Andrews shot back, "He was a soldier, boy. He knew what he was up against. Now, shut up and keep an eye out for them heathens."

We grew silent. From across the room came the sounds of whimpering children mixed with Rock-in-Hand's soothing voice.

I studied the ground between the station and the barn. The shadows were too thick and too dark to risk making a dash for the barn. Besides, the Paiutes could be waiting inside the barn. And I didn't want to chance using the tunnel. Not yet. It was always there as a last resort. "Our best bet is to stay right here until morning. Andrews is right. We could walk right into their hands." I glanced at Friday who squatted under the window with his back to the wall.

"Why don't you put us on some coffee, son? I reckon we could all use it."

I peered out the gun port, shivering. The westbound rider was due in a few hours. Somehow, he had to be warned. I said as much to Darcy as Friday handed me a cup of six-shooter coffee.

Andrews sneered. "Yeah, I bet you'd like to get out of here so you can turn the Army on us."

I glared at the corporal. The shadows playing over his thin face gave the appearance of a leering devil. "I ain't letting that boy ride in here and get himself killed. You don't trust me, then you go with me." I dropped my hand to the butt of my Colt. "Otherwise, you're going to have to stop me, and Mister, you ain't nowhere fast enough."

Darcy took a tentative step toward us.

Andrew's sneer broadened. "You don't know how good I am."

I grinned. "I don't have to. I know how good *I* am."

The air tingled with tension. Darcy broke in, "Back away, Corporal. Gabe here wants to warn the rider, let him be. We got the children and woman in here. He'll be back. I never known no Texan who wouldn't take on a grizzly for a woman and children."

"She ain't no woman." Corporal Andrews sneered. "She's just a squaw."

Darcy's eyes flashed fire. "Maybe she's just a

squaw, Corporal, but she is the lady who is taking care of the children Gabe's looking after. That makes a difference." He shook his head. "You got a heap to learn about folks, J. D. I hope you live long enough."

For several seconds, Darcy and I looked into each other's eyes. Like it or not, we were in this together. For the common good of all, we had to push aside any conflicting beliefs we held.

I gave him a brief nod. "I'd best go before the sun rises. I'll find me a little hidey-hole and wait. Bar the door after me. You'll know if anything happens." I glanced at Rock-in-Hands and the children, then turned to Darcy. "If something does happen to me, I'd appreciate you seeing that her and the children, and my boy, Friday, are taken good care of."

Darcy nodded. "Sure thing, Gabe."

After adjusting my ripper knife on my hip, I checked my Colt, then strung a Spencer over my back. The magazine was filled with seven cartridges. I carried an extra magazine in my pocket.

I felt a hand on my arm. It was Friday. He looked up at me, his dark eyes wide with fear. I grinned and tousled his hair. "Don't worry, boy. Everything's going to be just purty and peart."

I crossed to Rock-in-Hand. "Stay with the soldiers if something happens. They'll take care of you. I'll be gone a few hours."

She nodded, blinking back what I could have

sworn was the glitter of a tear in her eye. "I take care of the children. You not to worry."

I winked at her.

Peering out the gun port in the back window, I saw no movement. Slowly, I opened the back door a crack and peeked outside. The frigid air caught my breath.

Shadows covered the rear of the station. There were patches of darkness among the pines, stunted fir, sage and antelope brush. I studied them carefully, trying to discern shrub from human form. After a couple of minutes, I pulled my Colt and quickly stepped outside and crouched in the shadows against the wall.

I held my breath, expecting the impact of an arrow or lead slug at any moment. In my mind's eye, I could see dozens of Paiutes crouched in the pines, waiting for me. Despite the freezing temperatures, sweat beaded on my forehead. I tried to swallow, but my throat was too dry.

An owl hooted. I almost jumped out of my skin. "Easy, Gabe, easy," I muttered, my voice sounding oddly out of place in the crisp silence.

Seconds turned into minutes. I breathed easier. Rising to my feet, I eased along the rear of the station to the corner. Taking my time, I peered around the corner, searching the yard between the station and the barn.

Nothing.

Quickly, I moved to the other end of the station. The rider would be coming down the steep Kingsbury Grade from Daggett Pass. I had to head him off.

From the station, the trail led over rolling hills to the base of Kingsbury Grade. I planned to intercept the rider there.

I ghosted through the pines, my eyes constantly roving back and forth over the country ahead of me. The farther I got from the way station, the less I anticipated running into any marauding Paiutes.

Ahead protruded the granite ridge from which the mountain lion had leaped at George Wagner's horses. My first impulse was to crouch among the thick growth of sage around the base of the granite slab, but on second thought, I clambered to the top overlooking the trail and sprawled in the snow. I slid the Spencer in front of me and settled down to wait.

Slowly the eastern sky grew lighter. I shivered from the cold, wishing mightily for a cup of coffee or a shot of whiskey. The sun rose over Daggett Pass, a blinding ball of white against a deep blue sky.

About mid-morning, I heard voices. Half a dozen vague shadows materialized from the pine forest and found hiding spots in the new-growth fir and pine along the trail just beyond the ridge on which I lay.

My heart jumped into my throat when one Paiute pointed to my own hiding spot and started toward me. A sharp command halted him, and he melted back into the tangle of young pine bordering the trail.

The forest grew silent. From time to time, the chirp of a mountain chickadee or the screech of a hawk broke the stillness. Below, the waiting Indians had vanished into the landscape. I shivered, grateful for my heavy coat and wool clothing.

Time dragged. Had the rider run into trouble?

Suddenly, a voice drifted through the silence. I peered up the trail. A dark figure appeared around a bend.

I turned my attention to the Paiutes below. They were moving about, making ready to spring the ambush. Without hesitation, I pulled the Spencer to my shoulder and touched off a round at the warrior nearest the Express rider.

The Paiute screamed and staggered into the forest out of sight. Shouts of alarm echoed through the pine and fir. I emptied the magazine at the scrambling Paiutes crashing through the tall trees.

The dot on the trail remained motionless. I called out. "Paiutes. At the way station. Go around." My voice boomed across the valley on the frosty air.

The Express rider gave a wild shout and disappeared from the trail. Below, two dark figures moved in his direction. By the time I reloaded, they had faded into the pines.

Ignoring any danger, I slid down the ridge and

raced after the two, hoping to catch them before they intercepted the Express rider.

Moments later, I spied one brave racing through the pines ahead of me. I slid to a halt and snapped the Spencer to my shoulder. I fired, and the figure tumbled head over heels.

I raced past, heading toward where I thought the other Paiute should be, but within minutes, I knew I'd missed him. I hadn't heard any commotion, so I guessed the Express rider had made it safely around the station and was now on his way to Yank's. I turned back to the way station.

Now all I had to do was make it back inside. Easy to say, but hard to do with a band of wild Paiutes around.

I hadn't taken more than three steps when a heavy weight hit my shoulder and the point of a knife sent a sting of fire through my chest.

Chapter Nine

I twisted my shoulders when I saw the snow coming up to meet me. The sudden move swung the weight on my shoulders forward, throwing it to the ground. At the same time, I lunged forward, jamming my shoulder into my attacker. I rolled when I hit.

There came a sharp grunt.

We both jumped to our feet at the same time. A wiry Paiute brave stood glaring at me, a knife clutched in his hand. Before I could grab my own, he leaped, making a slashing sweep with the knife.

I jumped back, then feinted with my left, drawing him in that direction. As soon as he made his riposte, I threw a straight right that caught him behind the ear and slammed him to the ground.

In an instant, he was up, facing me, his face contorted with hatred. He lunged, swinging his arm overhead and bringing the knife straight down. I grabbed his wrist in an iron grip with both hands. The force of his blow drove me to my knees.

Standing over me, he threw his left hand over his right, using both to force the blade down. For long moments, we strained against each other, muscle against muscle, sinew pitched against sinew, determination pitted against determination. The rancid smell of his body stung my nostrils. His black eyes glittered with the fires of hate. Sweat beaded on his forehead.

I had never known an easy day in my life. From the time I was a boy able to ride, I worked like a hired hand for the families I lived with. At seventeen, I was tough as a dried mesquite post, and in the eleven years since, I hadn't put on an ounce of fat.

Slowly, I struggled to my feet, forcing the straining brave's hands up. He aimed a kick at my midsection, but the sudden fear in his eyes telegraphed the move. I yanked back and to the side, forcing him forward and into a spin.

He threw out a hand for balance, which gave me the split second advantage I needed to twist his knife hand up behind him and loop an arm around his throat. I squeezed.

He grunted and kicked back, trying to drive my

knee backward. I bent forward at the waist, forcing his legs to the ground. Clenching my teeth, I tightened my grip, choking off his breath and shutting down the flow of blood to his brain.

Within moments, he passed out.

I held him a few seconds after he went limp before releasing him. The Paiute warrior dropped to the ground. I grabbed his knife and held it to his throat.

I hesitated. I'd killed before, but only in self-protection—never a helpless jasper like this one, even if he was a renegade Paiute. Turning on my heel, I hurled his knife into the woods and relieved him of his ancient ball and cap pistol, which joined his knife among the pines. His old musket I busted against the closest tree.

Then I hurried back to the way station, taking care to remain in the underbrush.

At the edge of the clearing in front of the way station, I crouched against the scaly bark of a ponderosa. My heart thudded against my chest.

The sun lit the forest so brightly that it dazzled my eyes. I studied the forest around me. Nothing moved. I darted to a nearby tree and waited.

Had the Paiutes pulled out?

I couldn't believe it.

Suddenly, I glimpsed movement from the corner of my eye. I slid farther into the shadows of a pine and waited.

A dark figure glided through the pines from behind the way station and disappeared around the corner of the barn. A second, then a third followed, wraithlike shadows flitting through the pines.

Moving as quickly as I dared, I moved to a point where I could see what they were up to. I crouched and waited.

Moments later, a thin column of smoke arose from behind the barn. In the next second, a flaming arrow arced through the air, landing with a thump on the split shingle roof of the station. It was a futile gesture. Even though the snow had melted from the roof, the shingles were still wet. On the other hand, a single day with no moisture and a steady wind, the shingles would be tinder dry.

Hunkering down in the shadows, I waited and watched. After half a dozen arrows, the attempt ceased. I searched the forest around me, anxious to make my break for the way station, but wary of any sentries who might be watching.

I saw no one. The column of smoke grew thicker. I knew exactly where the Paiutes had taken refuge.

Thirty yards behind the barn curled a small stream that over the centuries had cut deeply into the soil between rugged layers of granite. On the north side of the stream was a natural windbreak, a horseshoe bank almost ten feet deep with a broad sand and gravel beach that allowed more than enough room for fire and blankets.

I guessed that to be the spot they had camped.

Moving slowly, I eased back to the west, remaining at the edge of the forest until I spotted the fire. I found a thick copse of young pine bent double by layers of snow. I slipped under the dome of branches and waited.

Moments later, I heard a grunt behind me. I froze, not daring to look around. The crunching sound of feet on snow reached my ears. I tightened my finger on the trigger of my Spencer, wishing I had my Colt in hand instead of the rifle. I held my breath, waiting for the sounds to halt.

They didn't.

Four Paiutes passed my hidey-hole, two on either side, but to my relief, far enough distant they paid me no attention.

Then I saw my chance to reach the cabin. The four were certain to garner attention when they entered the camp. If there were any sentries out, perhaps for a few moments, they would focus on the returning warriors.

As the four disappeared around the corner of the barn, I broke for the way station, staying low and hoping no one inside the station took a shot at me.

The door snapped open when I hit the porch, and I lunged inside.

Despite the closed shutters, the room was noticeably cooler because of the broken windows. The Rebs were each at a gun port. Rock-in-Hand and the bundled children were gathered on the hearth for warmth.

Darcy barked an order. "Andrews. Take my place here and keep a sharp eye on the barn. Those Paiute fellers are out behind it."

"They're camped in the bend of a creek. It makes a good windbreak," I said, opening my coat and shirt to inspect the knife wound. The cut was superficial, thanks to the thick wool mackinaw.

Darcy asked, "What about the rider?"

"I figure he made it around. I yelled at him."

Andrews growled from the darkness. "We heard." He hesitated. "How do we know you didn't yell for our benefit and then tell him we was here?"

I made out his head in silhouette against the window. "Because I'm telling you I didn't."

"That's enough, J. D. Keep your eyes on the barn." Darcy turned to me. "There's another rider due in this afternoon from the other direction. What about him?"

"The westbound will pass the word. He'll skirt the place here and keep on going around until they get word the Paiutes are gone."

"Well, that's something, I reckon."

I looked into Darcy's eyes. The red shadows from the fire flickered over his face. "The Express rider will send back help against the Paiutes when he reaches Yank's."

A crooked grin curled the broad-shouldered man's lips. "I figured as much."

His reply surprised me. "Then why'd you let me go out and warn him? You could have given yourself more time to get away."

"That ain't my way, Gabe. This here gold business has nothing to do with that kid on the pony. It's between me and them Abraham Lincoln lovers who will be coming after the gold." He hesitated and looked straight through me as he reflected. "Besides, I got a feeling a whole passel of boys is going to be pulled into this trouble before too long. And maybe what I'm doing here makes me responsible for a heap of them. I feel somewhat better knowing I at least saved one life."

Right then, I wished I didn't have a conscience. I wasn't committed to either side, or the gold. If Darcy could take such a chance to let that Express rider live, then I wanted to take a chance and help Darcy out of here.

But I couldn't. I had to notify the law. But then, I had an idea. "Well, I don't reckon you ought to wait around until help rides in. You boys had best beat a shuck out of here."

Andrews snorted. "You're forgetting about all them Paiutes out there."

"No." I shook my head. "I got me an idea how to spook them long enough to give us a chance to high-tail it out of here."

"Us?" Darcy arched an eyebrow.

I grunted. "You don't figure I'm staying behind with a woman and four children to face a war party, do you? No, sir. Like it or not, we're in this together."

Darcy chuckled. "What do you have in mind, Gabe?"

I pointed to the darkness at the end of the room. "I got boxes of .52-caliber paper cartridges for the Sharps. I figure we can rig up some bombs to throw amongst the Paiutes. Get their attention and then with four Spencers, we ought to be able to carve a big enough chunk out of their fighting men to make them pull back and reconsider the matter."

Private Henry spoke from the darkness on the other side of the room. "But, Sergeant. The wagon is full now with the gold. There's no room for anyone. Besides, I don't think our horses can pull the load up the hill Gabe has told us about."

I explained, "I wasn't thinking about your wagon. The man whose frozen carcass you found left a wagon down the road apiece. I got his four horses in the barn. We can transfer the gold and still have plenty room."

Darcy considered my idea. He studied me. "You don't think we can hold them off here?"

"I reckon we could. I don't reckon you would want that. You see, help will reach us. When it does, it's too late for you. And I don't want to take a chance on any of my people catching a stray slug."

Corporal Andrews came out of the darkness and stood in the flickering red shadows. Sarcasm coated his words. "Don't tell me you decided you want to wear Union blue."

"Not hardly, Corporal. I don't care about the gold you stole. You did me a favor by letting me warn the boy. Now, I'm returning the favor. It's up to you what to do with it. As far as I'm concerned, we're even now."

Andrews stomped forward. He threw out his chest. "We didn't steal it. We confiscated it for the South."

I glared at him. "No. There's no war, not yet. Maybe if there was, you could say that. But now, what you did was plain and simple stealing."

Darcy's calm voice cut in. "You going to turn us in, Gabe?"

For a moment, I hesitated. I respected Darcy for the compassion he had shown, so I owed him the truth. "I'll do what I can to help you out of here so none of my folks will be hurt. But if I have the chance to turn you in, I will."

He studied me a moment. "If there's anything I hate to come up against, it's principle. What if we take Friday with us and turn him loose when we leave Utah Territory? That'll stop you."

With a slow nod, I replied, "I reckon it would. So, what now?"

Darcy chuckled. "Well, Gabe, I'll tell you. Let's build those bombs, and you get us out of here. And then we'll see."

For the next hour, we tore open paper cartridges and packed black powder in canteens, glass medicine bottles, and empty whiskey bottles. For fuses, we soaked strips torn from a homespun shirt in coal oil and poked them down the necks of the containers.

Finally, we were ready.

Leaving Rock-in-Hand my Colt, I took Private Henry while Darcy took Andrews. One in each pair carried the Spencer at ready, the other five bombs with a Spencer strapped across his back.

I looked at Darcy. "When you're ready, whistle."

He nodded.

We slipped to either side of the barn.

Just as Henry and I reached the converted ambulance, the barn door opened. We ducked behind a wheel, keeping the wagon between the open door and us. I pulled my knife and motioned the private aside. I held my breath.

For several seconds, the Paiute sentry stood motionless, keeping the door between him and the way station. Every muscle in my body grew tense.

Leaving the door open to hide his retreat, the sentry dashed to the corner of the barn and disappeared.

He had no idea just how close he had come to dying.

Moments later, we paused at the corner around which he had vanished. Thirty yards away, he stood on the stream bank for a moment then leaped down out of sight.

I looked at Henry. "Ready?"

He drew the Spencer to his shoulder and nodded. I squatted and set my bombs on the ground. We had ten between us. That and four Spencers would spook anyone for a few hours.

I pulled a white phosphorus match from the waterproof pouch in my pocket.

A soft whistle came from the other end of the barn. I struck the match and touched it to the fuse.

The coal oil ignited and flared. I hurled the bomb through the air. In a blazing arc, it reached its apex, then dropped right into the middle of the camp.

Darcy's was right behind.

Chapter Ten

One explosion followed the other. White smoke billowed into the sky, and even before the Paiutes could move, we hurled more bombs into their camp.

With screams of fear and panic, the Paiute war party scattered like a covey of quail.

Corporal Andrews and Private Henry emptied their magazines into the billowing smoke. As soon as I threw my last bomb, I grabbed my Spencer and started firing.

Moments later, it was over.

Scattered along the bank of the creek, a few charred brands still burned, remnants of the fire. We found three dead Paiutes. Darcy shook his head. "With all the firepower we had, I expected more."

I scanned the dark woods surrounding us. "If we don't pull foot, they'll be back."

We found Private Melvin Cook in the barn, scalped. Private Henry muttered a soft curse. "Mel was a good boy. They didn't have to do that to him."

"We better get on with our business. We can't help him now," Andrews said.

"We can bury him." Private Henry glared at Andrews.

I nodded. "Yes. We can do that."

Andrews sneered. "How? The ground's frozen."

"Then we'll pile rocks on him, but we're going to bury Melvin." Joe Henry's eyes blazed with determination.

Rock-in-Hand approached. In a whisper, she said, "The young boy soldier in the station, he is dead."

We buried both young soldier boys, stacking rocks over them.

Afterward, we harnessed Wagner's four horses and led them back up the trail to the wagon. Using those four plus ours, we easily pulled the wagon back on the trail. We backed the team into place.

Darcy eyed the hastily repaired traces. "They going to hold?"

I shrugged as I swung into my saddle. "They don't, we'll patch them up again."

Thirty minutes later, we had transferred the gold and bundled the children in the bed of the wagon. By snugging the canvas top down good and tight over the oaken hoops, we made a cozy little refuge for the children.

Now all we had to do was get them up Kingsbury Grade and over Daggett Pass.

Kingsbury Grade was a series of switchbacks rising to the summit almost 1,100 feet above the South Tahoe Valley. In the spring of 1860, it replaced the dangerous Daggett Pass Trail.

The climb to the summit was formidable. Often stagecoach drivers made passengers walk, and now we were facing it with a load of children and gold with two feet of snow on the ground.

As we started our ascent to Daggett Pass, a new surge of gray clouds rolled in front of the afternoon sun.

The horses, two sorrels, a bay, and a dun, lowered their heads and leaned into their collars. I tossed a loop over the near wheel and tightened it around the axle. I dallied the other end to my saddle horn and helped pull the wagon. "Come on, Sam. Put some muscle in it," I mumbled to my pony.

Darcy followed my example, and with the two of us pitching in, the wagon groaned up the grade.

Corporal Andrews stayed out as scout, and although I'd had some black thoughts about him while Darcy and I were straining to pull the wagon, I forgot them all when he came racing in with word that the Paiutes were right behind him.

And they were. Screaming for blood!

A dozen howling warriors astride racing ponies rounded the bend and bore down on us. As one, Darcy and I threw the Spencers to our shoulders and began firing.

The lead Paiute somersaulted backward off his pony, causing the galloping horse behind to stumble and throw his rider. We poured a dozen more slugs into the melee charging us, then turned and raced for the wagon while Andrews and Henry covered us.

Private Henry had turned the wagon sideways in the trail, blocking any attempt by the Paiutes to race past and catch us in crossfire.

The Paiutes reeled in bewilderment before retreating around the bend. We settled down to wait. They would be back. We loaded our weapons. From the box of cartridges, I filled half a dozen magazines of .44s and dropped them in my pocket.

Then the snow hit.

I looked at the children. They huddled close to Rock-in-Hand who was cradling them to her under her blanket. She looked me in the eye. I knew what we had to do.

Turning to Darcy, I said, "Two or three switch-backs below is a cave. I've seen it from the trail. It looks large enough for the wagon and horses. It's our best chance for the night."

He looked at Andrews and Henry. The younger man shivered. Darcy nodded to me. "What about the Paiutes?"

"This weather, they'll fort up."

He nodded. "Take us there."

The snow grew heavier. By the time we reached the cave, I could scarcely see more than a few feet ahead of me.

The mouth of the cave was wide and low, so low we had to take the bows off the wagon to get it inside, but once inside, the cave opened into a large room. There was evidence of many fires. Dried limbs and logs lay scattered across the sandy floor of the cave.

Shadows filled the cave. The floor sloped slightly, so Darcy quickly built a small fire on the high side while Henry backed the wagon across the mouth of the cave and unhitched the horses. Leaving them in harness, we led them to a small room off the main cave.

While Friday put together a meal of bacon and beans and coffee, Private Henry and I headed out into the storm for firewood.

I couldn't help wondering about the Express rider out of Sacramento. He was somewhere out here in the middle of the storm with us. I sure hoped he made it through. Twenty-five dollars a week couldn't even begin to pay for the hardships those men faced.

We stumbled across several windfalls of pine and soon had a stack of wood that would last through the night. We even found some lighter pine, rock-hard pine shards still containing turpentine.

While we were gone, Corporal Andrews had rigged the canvas top across the mouth of the cave to keep out most of the random gusts of wind. Rock-in-Hand sat near the fire with her back to us as she fed the baby.

Mary and Phillip played in the dirt nearby.

Despite the gravity of our situation, we were snug and comfy. I warmed my hands at the fire, failing to notice that from time to time, the flames flickered toward an opening beyond the room in which we had stabled the horses.

Night fell over the countryside. Outside, the wind howled. Rock-in-Hand had the children by the fire, and as the evening wore on, one by one, they fell asleep.

I dozed. When I jerked awake much later, Darcy and Corporal Andrews had their heads together, trying to lay plans for the coming day. I chuckled to myself. With fresh snow to slow us down and a war party waiting to strike, there weren't too many plans they could develop that would solve anything. Our best bet was to sit and wait.

Corporal Andrews snorted when I suggested as much. "You'd like that, wouldn't you?" He glared at Darcy. "How do we know he hasn't already put out the word on us? He could have told that Express rider."

I shook my head in frustration. "I already told you once, Corporal." My eyes held his. "I don't lie, and I don't tolerate those who think I do."

Darcy stepped between us. "Back off, Andrews. Leave well enough alone." He turned to me. "You got any suggestions?"

"Nope. Truth is, Darcy, you old boys are in a predicament. We're all in a predicament, but you doubly so because of the gold. All I care about are the kids. For me and the children, the common sense thing is to sit tight until the storm passes, then try to make it to the Yosemite camp. At least there we've got someone to fight on our side."

"But suppose—"

In the middle of Darcy's question, I noticed the fire. From time to time, the flames leaped toward the opening beyond the horses.

My hopes surged. The only explanation was that somewhere in the rear of the cave, warm air was escaping. Maybe through a tiny fissure, or maybe even an opening large enough to take our horses out.

Darcy hesitated when he saw I wasn't listening. "What's going on?" His gaze followed mine to the shadows at the back of the cave.

"Look." I pointed to the fire.

All three men stared at the flames.

"So? What are we looking at?" Andrews growled.

Private Henry spoke up. "The flames. Fresh air is pulling them toward the back of the cave. There must be an opening back there." He looked at me with an expression of pride on his face. "Isn't that right?"

"That's right, boy. Somewhere back there is an opening. What we've got to do is find out where it goes, and if we can use it." I grinned at Darcy. "This might be how we get out of our predicament."

Leaving Corporal Andrews and Private Henry with Rock-in-Hand and the children, Darcy and I took a few pieces of lighter pine for torches and headed into the depths of the cave.

Less than fifty yards into the cave, I paused. "Look at that," I said, kneeling and holding the torch to several sets of horse tracks.

"What the blazes," Darcy muttered. "I wonder where this leads. Maybe there is a way out."

I rose and held the torch over my head. The cave was now about ten, maybe twelve feet wide. I tried to still the sudden surge of excitement pounding in my ears. "These mountains are millions of years old. No telling who lived here. Probably tribes that don't exist any longer." I looked at Darcy. "And who knows? You might be right. There might be another way out."

A flicker of surprise registered on his face, quickly replaced by a thoughtful frown. "You think there's a chance, Gabe?"

"Could be." I shrugged and stared at the tracks in

the sandy floor. A sandy floor? Where in the Sam Hill did the sand come from? We were in the middle of a granite mountain. We should have been standing on a granite floor. "Did you notice the floor?"

"Huh? What do you mean?"

"A sandy floor. You pay any attention to it?" Before he could reply, I continued. "This mountain is granite. The only way the sand could get in here is by water. Somehow, sometime, water flowed through here, bringing in sand from outside."

The frown on Darcy's face deepened. "You think there's a chance of a flood now?"

"I don't think it floods. Probably the snow melt. The water pulls sand from the fissures in the granite."

He shook his head. "Back home, we don't get much snow. How much would there have to be to push water through here?"

"Your guess is as good as mine. I'm from Jim Wells County in Texas. We see snow maybe once in a blue moon, if that."

I led the way, deeper and deeper into the cave.

Darcy spoke from behind. "Joe Henry is from Texas. Near Fort Worth. Mel was from Texas too."

"What about you and Andrews?"

"He's from Mobile, Alabama. My folks have a small plantation along the river near New Orleans. Raise indigo."

"You boys are widespread. How'd you all come to end up out here together?"

"The Fourth Louisiana. Henry run away from home after him and his stepfather had a fight. Andrews killed a man in Mobile, so Alabama wasn't too hospitable a place for him."

I peered into the darkness ahead. "What about you? Any ghosts in your past?"

He laughed. "Nope. My uncle organized the Fourth. Joining up was the thing for me to do. Them Yankee states seem intent on tearing down everything my family has worked to build for the last hundred and fifty years. We can't let them do that."

"You talk like there's a war going on now."

He grew serious. "Not right now, Gabe. But, you mark my words, one's coming, and it ain't going to be any fun-loving, rip-roaring paint the tiger. It's going to be savage as a meat axe." He paused. "One thing you're going to have to face, Gabe. You're going to have to take a side."

I snorted. "Don't bet your plantation on it."

Ahead the cave curved to the right. Falling silent, we plodded on. His words bothered me. If a fight came about, I wasn't taking any part of it. Let them that had something to gain do the fighting. All I wanted was enough money to buy a little spread up in Wyoming.

From time to time, a whiff of wood smoke reached us, a sure sign that a draft, however slight, was working through the cave. I lost track of time and distance.

Without warning, a faint gust of icy air struck my face. The flame on my torch whipped back and forth. "We're close!" I exclaimed, hurrying forward.

Ahead, the darkness of the cave gave way to the grayish light filtering down the passageway from the opening.

Chapter Eleven

We paused in the mouth of the cave and stared out over a snow-covered countryside that stretched for miles. The storm had passed. The sky was clear. From somewhere behind us, the rising sun cast an orange glow across the forest.

"You got any idea where we are?" Darcy muttered, standing at my side.

At my feet, the mountainside dropped off in a steep slope of sand and talus for almost a mile, at the end of which it butted into what appeared to be an old trail overgrown with two- and three-foot pine and fir.

At least fifty feet wide, the descent gave the appearance of a road leading away from the cave, except not even a fifty-mule team could pull a wagon up such a sharp grade.

"I'm not sure." I stared out over the carpet of swaying pines that undulated to the horizon, trying to orient myself to the lay of the land. Best I could figure, we were facing north, because the dim, angular shadows cast by the granite mountain lay before and to the left of us. "I think the way station is back to our left, to the west. And that old trail down there might be the old Daggett Pass Trail."

Darcy frowned. "The old trail?"

"Yeah. The trail we came up is the new one. They opened it last spring. The way I understand the story is that the old Daggett Pass Trail was the route used early on by the Pony Express. But it was too dangerous and too long. That's why some hombre named Kingsbury built the road we came up on. Cut off about fifteen miles from Sacramento to Carson City."

Pointing down the slope with his torch, Darcy grunted. "We'll never get the wagon down that slope."

He was right. We had walked hours for nothing. "Then I guess we'd better get back."

At that moment, a muffled sound echoed through the cave. I looked at Darcy. "You hear that?"

"I heard something. I'm not sure what."

We turned back.

I lost track of time, but after a time, I noticed the sandy floor growing spongy. Water was seeping in. The closer we came to the main room, the thinner the consistency of the sand, until we were sloshing through an ankle-deep syrup of sand and water.

When we reached the main room, I jerked to a halt. Darcy stopped at my shoulder and gaped. "What the—" he exclaimed.

The wagon was missing.

I looked around. At the high spot in the room, Rock-in-Hand sat by the fire with the children huddled behind her. Mary peeked around the Indian woman's side.

Covered by a blanket, a figure lay motionless in front of the fire.

Darcy and I exchanged confused looks before sloshing through the sandy slurry to the fire. Rock-in-Hand rose, and Friday raced to meet me.

Private Henry lay unconscious on the sand next to the fire.

Friday hugged me around the waist with his one arm. "Gabe. I am glad you come back." He motioned to Rock-in-Hand. "We both happy. Now we be safe."

Darcy knelt by Henry and pulled back the blanket to reveal a bloodstained shirt. He'd been shot in the chest. "What happened?" He looked up at the Washoe woman.

Friday pointed to the mouth of the cave. "The other one. He want to take wagon. They argue and the other one, he shoot this one. Then he take wagon and run horses away."

I looked around for Sam, my buckskin pony. He was nowhere to be seen.

Fire blazed in Darcy's eyes when he glared up at me. "That no-good . . ."

He cursed J. D. Andrews, but no worse or more vehemently than I cursed the corporal.

Private Henry's anguished moan interrupted our angry tirade. Darcy bent over the young man. "The bullet's still in there. We've got to cut it out."

I stared at the back of his head. "We? I've never cut on a man. What about you?"

Darcy sat back on his heels. He pushed his hat to the back of his head, and sweat ran down his face. "No."

Rock-in-Hand rose and handed me the baby. She held out her hand to Darcy. "Give me knife."

For a moment, he hesitated.

"I care for many warrior."

I shrugged at him. "Somebody's got to do it."

Darcy continued to hesitate.

"I trust her," I said.

He handed her the knife, which she inspected, then returned to him. "Make sharp. I make water hot." Taking a pot, she waded through the water and sand slurry to the mouth of the cave where she packed snow into the pot.

She scooted it into the coals, and the heat quickly melted the snow. By the time Darcy had put an edge on the blade, the water was boiling. I stood aside, holding the sleeping baby and watching. From beyond the fire, Friday and the two children looked on.

Rock-in-Hand tested the edge of the knife with her thumb, nodded her approval, then swished it in the boiling water to remove any particles of metal remaining from the sharpening. Taking a piece of wool she had cut from the blanket, she soaked it in the hot water and cleaned the wound and surrounding flesh.

Bright red blood oozed from the wound. Private Henry groaned. Sweat stood out on his face and forehead.

"At least it missed the lungs," I muttered, setting my jaw in anticipation of what was to come.

Darcy's face was white as the snow. "What can I do?"

She gestured to Henry's hands. "Hold down." She looked up at me. "Give Friday baby. You sit on the young soldier's legs."

We did as she instructed. She placed a short branch between Henry's teeth. "Bite," she commanded Joe Henry, straddling his waist. To us, she said, "Hold tight."

That was one of the most bizarre situations in

which I have ever found myself. There we were in a cave with me sitting on a boy's legs, a Johnny Reb wearing the union blue of the U.S. Army holding his hands, an Indian woman digging out a bullet, four children watching from the fireside, and a twenty-foot wide swath of snow-melt water two inches deep coursing through the cave.

Rock-in-Hand deftly wielded the knife.

A guttural groan ripped from the young man's throat. He arched his back, lifting Rock-in-Hand off the ground before collapsing into unconsciousness.

She worked quickly. Within a minute, she held up the bloody slug, tossed it to Darcy, then cleaned the wound and sprinkled some powder from her par-fleche bag on it before wrapping it with a clean rag. "Now, he must rest." She gestured to the cavernous room, then hugged herself. "Not good for hurt man. Cold. Cold not good for wound."

Darcy indicated the fire. "That can make him warm. Isn't that enough?"

She shook her head sharply. "Need teepee, home. Keep out wind and chill. Go back to horse station." She pointed down the mountain.

Darcy protested, "I'm going after Andrews. I'm not letting him get away with that gold."

I rose and brushed the sand from my trousers. "I don't blame you, but first things first. Rock-in-Hand is right. Henry will be better off back at the station. We can outwait the Paiutes until help gets there."

Darcy chewed on his bottom lip. His gaze kept going to the open mouth of the cave. I knew the unsettling concern coursing through his brain. With every minute wasted, the traitor Corporal J. D. Andrews was getting farther and farther away with the gold.

I had the feeling that Darcy would make the right decision. He seemed a decent man although we didn't share the same convictions. But even if he decided to leave us to pursue Andrews, I was taking all the others back to the station, even if I had to carry Henry on my back.

The late-afternoon sun shone through the mouth of the cave, bathing the interior in a red glow. Rising, Darcy slogged through the sandy slurry to the mouth of the cave.

The wagon tracks leading up Kingsbury Grade were quickly melting away as the snow melt from above washed down the slope and into the cave. "How far do you figure we are from the way station?"

"Maybe four miles."

"How long to get there?"

"On foot—three, four hours."

He looked up the grade toward the summit of the mountain. "All the while, Andrews is getting farther and farther away."

"Maybe so, but at the station, you can get yourself a pony. Here, you're on foot, and if the Paiutes hap-

pened onto you in that condition, you'd be as helpless as a newborn calf."

Rock-in-Hand took the baby from Friday and
squatted by the children. I smiled at her. "Thanks."

She smiled briefly, her white teeth a sharp contrast
to her dusky complexion. She nodded toward the
fire. "Eat."

The snow continued melting, keeping a steady
stream of water flowing through the cave.

Darcy turned to face us. He shook his head. "We
can't make it tonight. Let's pull out at first light."

"Sounds good to me," I replied, reaching for my
knife and heading outside.

"What now?" Darcy frowned at me.

I hooked a thumb toward Private Henry. "A travois to get him down."

He grinned at me. "You scare me, Gabe."

Now he had me puzzled. "How's that?"

"You're always thinking. That could be dangerous."

Like I said, in another situation, in another time,
Darcy and me could have turned out to be the best
of friends.

We kept the fire roaring throughout the night. The
flow of water slowed as the frigid temperatures froze
the snow, but come mid-morning, the melt would
continue again.

After a hasty breakfast, we laid the wounded

young man on the travois and covered him best we could. We had rigged a double harness for Darcy and me. The children were bundled with only an opening for their eyes. Rock-in-Hand would carry the infant in her arms and Mary on her back. Friday would carry Phillip.

Before we left the cave, we checked our weapons just in case the Paiutes happened upon us. I laid my hand on Friday's shoulder. "You sure you can handle it, boy?"

He grinned up at me. "I do it, Gabe. Not to worry. I do good job for Mr. Willam H. Russell."

I laughed and scrubbed his head with my hand. "You bet you will." I turned at Rock-in-Hand. "If you get tired, call out. I'd sooner we rest and get there later than go full chisel and tucker plumb out."

"I—the children and I will not—" She hesitated. She screwed up her face, searching for the right words. "As you say—tucker plumb out."

I studied Rock-in-Hand for several moments. She matched me eyeball-to-eyeball. There was a fine woman. I nodded and slipped into the harness. "Well, Darcy, you ready? The sooner we get started, the sooner you can get after Andrews."

He cursed the corporal once again and then said, "Let's get the blazes out of here."

The first mile was the hardest for we had to break through the hard crust the frigid night had put on the snow. As the sun warmed the snow, walking became easier.

Towering pines and fir bordered the trail, and from time to time, we'd pull off the trail and back into the forest for a brief rest.

As the snow continued to melt, the ground grew soggy. "One thing for certain," Darcy said, looking over our back trail. "We can't hide from nobody. We best hope them Paiutes don't come along."

He was right. Our backtrail was a mixed set of footprints and drag marks, all giving mute, but obvious, evidence of our passage.

After two hours, we were within a couple miles of the station. The sky remained clear, the sun hot. Despite the chill, sweat stung my eyes and ran down my spine.

"How'd you come to end up with that Injun boy you call Friday?" Darcy kept his eyes forward.

I leaned into the rope harness. "I thought I told you."

He grunted and wheezed. "Might have. Tell me again. Helps pass the time."

Between gasps of breath, I replied, "He showed up last September. Skinnier than a pine shoot—the stub of his arm infected. He was about two hoots and a holler from taking up a patch of ground. I reckon one of my failings is that I couldn't even turn a mangy old hound dog away, so I brought him in." I chuckled, thinking back to that night. "I'd whipped up a pot of elk stew and dumplings. That boy must've put himself around four or five plates. Why, his belly stuck out like one of those balloons that haul folks around the sky. Next morning when I woke up, he had the fire going and the coffee on."

Darcy chuckled. "Sort of just moved in, huh?"

"Reckon so."

"That name, Friday. That's an odd one. Seems like I read about someone named that once."

"Well, it ain't after the name of this place here, Friday's Station. Nope, it came from a book I read. A man named Defoe. Had a man named Robinson Crusoe stranded on an island and this native jasper showed up. Well, old Crusoe, he named this native Friday. So when this little Paiute boy showed up, I figured Friday was good enough for him. Besides, I couldn't pronounce his Indian name."

Darcy chuckled. He glanced over his shoulder. "How you doing back there, Joe?"

Between clenched teeth, the young soldier muttered. "Peart as can be, Sergeant. Peart as can be."

I grinned at the boy's grit. He didn't sound peart, but he had grit. "Just hold on, boy. Another couple of hours."

Chapter Twelve

The minutes dragged. Despite the cold, sweat poured down my lanky body, soaking my clothes. My legs ached. Darcy gasped for each breath. We fell silent, nearing exhaustion. The only sounds breaking the icy silence were strained grunts and the sloshing and sucking of our feet in the muddy ground, occasionally punctuated by the sharp tap of the travois striking a rock beneath the mud.

The trail began leveling off. A surge of hope boosted my spirits, for in the distance I made out the spearhead-shaped ridge just this side of the way station. I glanced at Rock-in-Hand slogging along beside us, the infant cradled in her arms and the boy fastened to her back. "Not long now. Just beyond that granite slab."

She didn't smile, but I saw a soft look in her eyes I had not noticed before. "Good. The children are tired."

Ahead, a horse's whinny broke the icy silence.

Darcy and I exchanged an anxious look. I nodded to a tangle of young pine and fir at the edge of the trail. "Maybe we best fort up in there and take a look. I'd hate to stumble onto a roomful of Paiutes."

Ten minutes later, Darcy and I knelt behind the scaly bark of a ponderosa pine and studied the way station. It appeared deserted. I pointed to the far end of the cabin. "Let me get down there. If any of them Paiutes are inside, we'll get them in a crossfire."

Staying close to the rear wall of the station, I ducked under the window and hurried to the far corner. At the corner, I gestured for Darcy to wait, then slid along the wall until I reached the window. I cocked my handgun and leaned forward, just enough to peer around the window jamb.

Empty.

I studied the barn. Another whinny sounded, this time from inside the barn. An answering nicker came from the forest across the clearing, and a wiry little bay emerged from the new growth of pine and fir at the edge of the forest. I watched as the pony trotted slowly to the barn, nosed open the door, and disappeared inside.

The place appeared deserted.

I waved at Darcy, pointing to the front door.

He nodded.

Ducking under the window, I eased to the corner and peered around it. Darcy stood at the far end of the cabin.

He dipped his head at the door.

Every sense alert, I moved along the porch. We met at the door. He looked at me, flexed his fingers about the butt of his handgun, and reached for the door bar.

I nodded, and he jerked the bar up and slammed the door open. We leaped inside, ready to fire.

The station was empty.

The interior looked like a prairie tornado had swept through it, furniture overturned, dishes and pots strewn about the room, bunks broken.

But the rugged way station still stood, its thick pine walls and solid roof intact. "Let's see about the animals," I said, heading for the door.

All the stock had been turned loose, but half a dozen head had meandered back in the barn against the icy winds and snow of the previous day.

Quickly bridling two mustangs, we hurried back to Rock-in-Hand and the others. Within minutes, we had the entire party inside the station.

Friday stoked the coals in the fireplace while Darcy and I fed and tended the ponies in the barn. I glanced at him. "I reckon you're bent on pulling foot as soon as you can. Give us time to wrap up a package of grub. A few more minutes won't hurt nothing."

He studied the bay he was feeding. "This one looks like a stayer. You got no objection, Gabe, I'll take him."

Suddenly, the barn grew dark. I peered outside as clouds pushed past the sun. A single flake of snow landed on my cheek. "Uh-oh. Looks like another storm coming. You might ought to wait till morning."

Darcy stopped at my side, his eyes narrowing as he saw the clouds scudding overhead. "I'll make it back to the cave for the night. Then I can push out in the morning."

I could see there was no arguing with him. "Come on in and get some grub."

He cleared his throat. "Is it okay if I leave Joe Henry here?"

I shook my head as if to say that was a foolish question. "You bet. The boy'll be fine just like he was in his own bed. Now, let's get inside. We've got to bundle you enough grub for the next few days."

He nodded. "Like I said, Gabe. You're always thinking."

We stared at each other a moment. I cleared my throat. "Look, Darcy. I'm not interested in the gold, and like I said, I want no part of the trouble you say's coming. But you got my gratitude and thanks for helping us get back here." I offered him my hand.

Darcy eyed me a moment. "You still plan on turning us in to the law?"

"I don't know. I honest-to-goodness don't know."

He stepped forward and took my hand. "Thanks, Gabe. I won't blame you if you do. But as to this war that's coming—whether you like to or not, I'm afraid the trouble is going to pull you in, just like it's already pulled so blasted many of us in. I hope I'm wrong. You're a good man. I'd like to see you get that ranch up in Wyoming."

Inside, Friday had a fire blazing. Coffee was starting to boil in a stewpot and several venison steaks were broiling from the spit over the fire.

Rock-in-Hand had gathered the children on the hearth, warming them.

While we sat around the sawbuck table and put ourselves around the grub, Darcy asked what I planned to do about the children.

I grinned sheepishly at Rock-in-Hand. "Well, since I got her to help with them, I can afford to wait out the winter. The next Express rider that comes through, I'll send word to Sacramento that I have them. Maybe there's a good family to take 'em in."

Darcy shrugged. "You can always send them to one of those orphan homes. They'll take kids with no family."

I shook my head. "No. I was an orphan. I know what it's like not to have someplace to call home." I studied the children—Friday, Mary, Phillip, and the infant in Rock-in-Hand's arms. I half-joked, "Why, I'd be tempted to keep them myself before I'd turn them over to one of those orphan homes."

Darcy arched an eyebrow. "You? I thought you was going up to Wyoming."

I grinned. "I reckon so. Last I heard, kids can grow up in Wyoming just like they can in Texas."

He chuckled. "Reckon they can, Gabe. Reckon they can."

The threatened storm never materialized. Darcy grinned broadly as he packed his gear on his bay. "Maybe luck's smiling on me, Gabe. Looks like a clear night. I'll reach the cave and go from there tomorrow." He swung into the saddle and looked down at me.

I extended my hand. "Take care."

He winked and shook my hand. "You too."

And then he rode off, disappearing into the night.

I might go to Hades for it, but I hoped him the best of luck.

Just after sunup, Friday and I readied the Express rider's pony just in case he made it in. I figured the snow might have melted some at Daggett Pass, but even if it hadn't, those determined young men would find a way around, over, or through. And I wanted to be ready for them.

Inside, Mary and Phillip slept peacefully on a pallet near the fire, as did the infant in its warm box. Private Henry stirred in his bunk. Rock-in-Hand sat quietly beside the children, punching holes in deerskin.

Friday poured himself a cup of coffee and sat at the table. I leaned back in a straight-back chair near the fireplace and rolled a cigarette.

Rock-in-Hand looked up from her handiwork. "You mean what you say to soldier man about children?"

I frowned momentarily, then realized what she meant. I had to chuckle. "I don't know if I did or not. What with their ma and pa being dead . . ." My words drifted off as I considered just what I should do. Then I nodded. "Yes. I'd keep them until we could find their family back East. I reckon there's a grandma or uncle or aunt somewhere."

She studied me thoughtfully, her large dark eyes searching mine. "If there be no family?"

"Huh? Oh, well, I'm right certain they got family. It might take some months to find 'em, but we will. I could keep the kids right here. This job is mine until I leave. But . . ." I grinned sheepishly at her. "I'd sure need you to stay and help."

"Do you forget cattle drive?"

I grimaced. I had forgotten about it. But maybe I

could work something out with my relief at the way station. There was no reason she and the children could not remain here with the new stationmaster until the family came for the children. "Yeah. I forgot, but I think I know how to solve the problem."

She frowned. "Sol-solve?"

"Make right. Make good everything."

Her eyes grew serious. "Then I stay."

I flicked the cigarette stub into the fireplace. "Good. That's settled."

Or so I thought.

Chapter Thirteen

The westbound rider was Johnny Fry. He came on schedule. According to him, the search for the stolen gold had moved east of Carson City. I just shrugged and kept my mouth closed, feeling guilty for keeping quiet about Darcy and the gold.

After he departed, I checked the horses once again, then went inside where I made sure the window shutters would close and lock, and the two remaining Spencers were loaded.

I plopped down at the sawbuck table and rolled a cigarette. Silently, Rock-in-Hand glided to my side with a cup of coffee. "Thanks."

Squatting nearby, she said nothing, but her presence filled me with a strange warmth and contentment. Often in my wandering, I'd pull up on hilltops at night and stare down at the lighted windows of distant ranch houses. I'd wonder how it felt to be inside one of those houses, and now I knew; now I realized the comfort, the security, and the satisfaction of being part of a family. At least, in a small way.

She continued working on the deerskin in her hands.

"What are you making there?"

She smiled up at me and held up a tiny deerskin jacket, a slipover. "For the baby," she said softly, her voice filled with the love and pride a mother has for her child.

"What of your own child?"

Her eyes grew sad. "The coughing sickness. She not strong."

"Where is your husband?"

She shook her head slowly. "He fight with soldiers against Paiute. He killed. No warrior want me. That is why Ten-ie-ya, the chief of the Yosemite, send me with you."

"What happens when you go back?"

She turned her attention back to the tiny deerskin jacket and continued lacing the side. "They not take me back. I am outcast to them."

I grimaced and stared at the children. I thought about George Wagner lying dead up the trail. I needed to do something for him, but I couldn't take the chance of leaving Rock-in-Hand alone with the children in case the Paiutes returned. I'd have to do it when I could.

Rock-in-Hand had obviously grown tired of Friday's daily menu of venison, gravy, and biscuits, so she whipped up some sort of meat pie, a bowl of succotash, and a pudding dessert in which she had mixed molasses, sugar, and some spices with the rest of the fixings.

We all sat at the table about four that afternoon. Whatever spices she used filled the way station with a sharp, sweet smell that in itself could just about satisfy a jasper's hunger.

Joe Henry was pale, but he had a grin on his face when he sniffed the pudding. He struggled to his feet and shuffled to the table.

"You sure you feel strong enough to sit at the table? You can take supper in bed." I looked at him in concern.

He shook his head. "I'm fine."

We proceeded to do justice to the repast. Even Phillip and Mary joined in with gusto, the first time they were truly animated since their ma and pa had gone away. I washed the last of my pudding down with strong coffee and reached for my bag of Bull Durham.

As an afterthought, I crossed the room to the station desk and opened the bottom drawer. The full bottle of Monongahela whiskey was still there, so I carried it back to the table where I poured Joe and me a short drink in our empty coffee cups. I lit my cigarette and sighed in satisfaction. "That was a right fine meal, Rock-in-Hand." I patted my belly. "I reckon I'll sleep like a baby tonight."

Outside a horse whinnied. Seconds later, boot heels thumped on the porch. I shucked my Colt and in two steps reached the door.

There came a knock, then a voice. "Gabe. It's me, Darcy. Let me in."

Fumbling with the locking peg, I opened the door. "What are you doing back?"

His gaze darted to the empty bed, then to the table where Joe Henry grinned at him. "Hello, Sergeant," said the young man.

"You never answered me. What are you doing back here? You find Andrews?"

He spotted the bottle of whiskey on the table. I grinned and nodded. He poured a drink, sipped it, then sighed. "Long time since I tasted that. About Andrews, I didn't find him, but I found the wagon. It went off the road and is in the bottom of a canyon. I'm guessing he left it there and went on in to Carson City to bring back help."

"Makes sense to me."

"That's why I'm here. I need your help to get the gold out of the canyon. I figure we can break open the barrels and just bring the bags up."

"I'll help, Sergeant." Joe Henry tried to stand, but sat down weakly on the bench.

Rock-in-Hand rose quickly and laid her hands on his shoulders. "No. He is weak. He must rest. No help." She fixed her eyes on Darcy, daring him to dispute her.

For a moment, he tried to outstare her, but finally dropped his gaze. He glanced sidelong at me. "What about it, Gabe? If I get it loaded and out of here before he gets back, he's got no reason to bother you. Maybe he'll figure the Paiutes found it."

"You're dreaming, Darcy," I replied, my voice heavy with sarcasm. "If the gold's gone, and he can't find you, he'll come here." I muttered a curse. "Looks like whether I want it or not, I'm caught up in this mess of yours."

He glanced at Rock-in-Hand, chastened by my words. "You're right, of course, but will you help?"

"I don't see that I've got a choice. If I do, then you owe me."

His eyes narrowed.

I read his thoughts. "Don't worry about your gold. I want you to take me to the dead man you ran across up the trail. I want to bring him back. I have to find his family so I can send them the children."

He grinned. "Then let's go bring him back. We got some daylight."

The eastbound express rider was due within an hour. "Friday here could handle the afternoon rider, but I'm not all-fired anxious to travel out there at night. We'll leave at first light. That'll put us back here by noon without trouble."

Darcy grimaced. He cut his eyes up Kingsbury Grade.

"Same with the gold. We'd never reach it before dark."

Reluctantly, he nodded.

I gestured to the table. "Why don't you sit and put yourself around some of Rock-in-Hand's grub. It'll stick to your ribs like mud on a hog."

Leaving the Spencers with Rock-in-Hand and Joe Henry, we pulled out before sunrise. An hour and a half later, we found George Wagner. He lay sprawled facedown, stiff as a plank. He was so rigid, we couldn't even straighten his arms or legs, so we had to spend some time building a travois to haul him back.

As we approached the way station, I had Darcy ride ahead and make sure the children didn't see me bring their pa in. I waited at the edge of the forest as he went inside. Moments later, he reappeared and waved me forward.

Between the two of us, we got Wagner inside the smokehouse and laid him on a plank next to the casket that held his wife. I fished through his pockets for papers, anything to help run down their family.

I glanced up at Darcy. "After we get your gold, I'll build him a casket."

The broad-shouldered Reb grinned. "My gold, Gabe? What about Lincoln? I thought you said it was his gold?"

I shook my head in frustration. "I don't know, Darcy. Everything is getting mighty confused."

He laughed. "I know." His gaze settled on the frozen face of George Wagner, then drifted to the casket at his side. He grew serious. "Let's build the casket now, Gabe. The gold can wait."

Well, right then, I was mighty glad that I knew Sergeant Paul Darcy.

By dark we had finished the casket, but we couldn't fit George Wagner in it, not in his frozen state. "Now what?" Darcy frowned.

I was puzzled. We couldn't take the poor jasper inside to thaw him out in front of the children. "Only thing I know is build a fire in here."

He nodded to the other casket. "What about her?"

I couldn't believe the ghoulish turn our conversation had taken. "Maybe she won't thaw too much."

So we built a fire and thawed George Wagner enough to fit him in his casket.

After I nailed the lid tight, we stepped back and stared at the two caskets.

A strange emptiness filled my chest. "I don't reckon when those two started out they ever had any idea they'd end up here."

Darcy grunted. "At least they're still together. What are you going to do with them?"

I fished the bag of Bull Durham from my pocket and rolled a cigarette, then tossed Darcy the bag. "I suppose if their family doesn't say something before it warms up, I reckon I'll just have to bury them out here." I looked up, seeing not the overhead joists in the smokehouse roof, but the stately pines and blue sky beyond. "If an hombre has to be buried, this is as pretty a place as I know."

That night, I looked through the papers I had taken from George Wagner. There was the name of a banker in Sacramento along with a bankbook indicating the Wagners had almost two thousand dollars on deposit.

I wrote a letter to the banker, planning on giving it to the westbound the following morning. Any youngsters with a two-thousand-dollar inheritance were bound to have family somewhere.

Next morning, leaving Friday to take care of the express rider, we headed up Kingsbury Grade, leading four ponies on which we'd rigged *aparejoes*, Mexican packsaddles.

Halfway up, we met Bob Haslam from Genoa Station. I gave him the letter to the banker. "Friday's got your pony ready."

"And some coffee, I hope." He laughed.

I nodded. "And some coffee."

With a whoop and a wave, Bob wheeled his pony and raced down Kingsbury Grade.

The wagon was where Darcy had said, in a canyon by Daggett Pass. The wind cut through our clothes like a straightedge razor, taking our breath away. I reckoned that was to be expected when a jasper reaches 7,300 feet.

To the east, we could see Carson Valley a few thousand feet below.

We tied our ponies to some stunted fir, and Darcy tossed a couple of lines down the steep slope. Grabbing the canvas bags we had fashioned the night before with Rock-in-Hand's help, he paused before heading down. "I'll fill 'em and you bring them up."

"How much you have down there?"

"A dozen barrels. Each one has about twenty ten-pound bags of gold dust."

I whistled. "That's quite a load. Maybe you ought to take my horse and spread it around. I can make it back to the way station on foot."

"Thanks, but I can make it with my five."

Holding one of the ropes, he slipped and slid down the steep slope to the wagon. He uncovered the barrels, and using the butt of his Colt, split the top of the first one. Quickly, he loaded five bags of gold, a hundred pounds. "Okay. Take it up."

I looped my end of the rope around the saddle horn and urged my pony forward. The canvas bag slid over the snow easily. When it reached the top, I loaded the gold onto the first pack horse, then tossed the canvas bag back to Darcy.

Twenty-one more times we slid the canvas bags up, but each time, the weight of the bag displaced more snow until we were dragging them over the jagged granite. With one barrel left, the canvas bags fell apart, so Darcy and I had to lug the last twenty bags of gold up the steep slope.

Gasping for breath, we leaned against our ponies. "That's too much like work," he said, laughing.

I agreed.

Darcy checked the ropes holding the gold. Satisfied they were snug, he swung into the saddle and looked down at me. "Well, Gabe. Reckon this is it." He extended his hand.

We shook. "You keep your eyes working, Darcy. A heap of folks want what you got there."

He looked past my shoulder at the valley below. A tiny trickle of smoke rising into the air marked the location of the way station. "What are you going to tell J. D. if he comes back?"

I grinned. "What can I tell him? You forced me to help you load up and then you rode out."

"Good luck. And take care of Joe for me."

"Don't worry about that boy. He'll be up and around before you know it."

Chapter Fourteen

We parted at the top of Daggett Pass, Darcy heading down into Carson Valley, me back to Friday's Station. I wasn't too concerned about J. D. Andrews showing up. With two Spencers and a Sharps backing me, he was the least of my worries, even with a handful of hombres behind him.

The sun was dropping behind the ponderosa pines as I rode in. Friday met me on the porch and followed me to the barn where we readied a fresh black mustang for the eastbound at six o'clock and tied him in the holding shed.

Inside, Private Joe Henry was sitting up, laughing and teasing Mary and Phillip. Rock-in-Hand sat nearby, a blanket over her shoulders as she nursed the infant. Joe looked up. His eyes asked the question.

I winked. "He's on his way, boy. And the weather is prime. He ought to be down in Carson Valley by now and heading for Santa Fe."

A distant shout galvanized me into action. I grabbed my hat. Friday beat me to the door. A flying pony bore down on us, snow and mud flying from its hooves. A young man shouted and waved as he jerked the horse to a sliding halt.

"Howdy, Gabe, Friday," Johnny Fry said, whipping the *mochila* off his spent pony and slapping the leather bags on the black.

Friday handed him coffee, and I slipped a bundle of grub in his saddlebags. "Look out for yourself going over the pass, Johnny. I hear there's some old boys out there searching for that Union gold."

He gave me a devil-may-care grin and swung into the saddle. "They best give me room. I'm a rip-snorting, caterwauling wildcat from deep in the hills. I was raised by she-wolves and cut my teeth on grizzly bear." He grinned down at Friday. "You believe that, boy?"

Friday smiled up at me and nodded. "I believe it."

"I do too, son." I laughed and looked back to Johnny Fry. I decided to take some precautions in case J. D. Andrews showed up. "There could be a heap of trouble going on hereabouts, Johnny. Pass the word to the westbound to fire three shots coming in. If you don't get a three shot answer, swing around the station."

He nodded. "Take care, Gabe."

"You too, Johnny."

Well before sunup, a banging at the door jerked me from a sound sleep. I grabbed my Colt and peered through a crack in the shutters. I blinked and looked again. All I saw was a shadow. "Who's there?" I called through a gun port.

"It's me, Gabe. Darcy."

Darcy!

I threw up the bar and yanked the door open. "What the blazes you doing here now? I figured you would already be halfway to Santa Fe."

He glanced over his shoulder and staggered inside. The flickering firelight illuminated his haggard face. I stuck my head out the door. I couldn't see his horse.

He stumbled to the fire and dropped to his knees, warming his hands. He shivered. "It was J. D. I saw them coming across Carson Valley. I knew I couldn't outrun them, so I turned back." He went into a paroxysm of shivers so violent his teeth clacked.

Rock-in-Hand quickly crossed the room and helped him remove his heavy coat. She then draped a wool blanket over his shoulders, and Friday handed the shaking man a cup of steaming coffee.

"I pour whiskey in it," the boy said to me. "It help warm him."

After a few minutes, the shivering subsided. I'd lit the lantern, and in the light, Darcy looked as if he'd aged ten years. "What happened? Where's your horse?"

He glanced toward Daggett Pass. "Back up there with the others. I backtracked and hid them and the gold before J. D. spotted me. He's riding with ten or twelve mighty rough-looking hombres."

Joe Henry frowned. "What if they find the gold, Sergeant? What then?"

Darcy gave us a crooked grin. "They won't. I pulled part of the mountain down around the gold and sent the horses running. I been wandering the forest ever since. Got myself lost once or twice."

Rock-in-Hand placed a bowl of steaming corn mush in Darcy's hands. The near-frozen man gobbled it like it was a Kansas City steak.

I studied Darcy while he put himself around the mush. I couldn't figure where he hid the gold, and I didn't want to ask. The gold was his business, him and J. D.'s. Somehow, I felt a little less guilty not knowing where it was.

Joe and I exchanged glances. The same thought had occurred to both of us. I cleared my throat. "That means he'll come here."

Darcy hesitated, then looked up at me, his face somber. "That's why I came back, Gabe. You folks are in this mess because of me. I don't reckon on running out on you."

Rock-in-Hand offered me a cup of coffee. I smiled at her. "Thanks." She ducked her head shyly and hurried back to the baby.

I sat at the table, studying our situation. Joe sat across from me. "You got any ideas, Gabe?"

"Maybe," I replied. "Just maybe."

We needed a hole card, a surprise that might just tip the upcoming fight in our favor. Once again, we turned to the paper cartridges, building a few small bombs. Darcy frowned when he saw them. "Where's the fuse?"

"Right here." I tossed him a small box.

He caught it deftly. "What's this?"

"Percussion caps. They're touchy little fellers."

His frown deepened.

I explained, "We drop a couple of handfuls of percussion caps in each bomb, which we'll then place in the most likely spots those hombres will hide. We'll cover them with snow or mud to disguise them. The impact of the slug will set off the percussion caps, which in turn will detonate the powder."

Joe's face lit with understanding. "That ought to make some of them hightail it out of here."

Darcy arched a skeptical eyebrow. "Will it work?"

I tore open some more cartridges. "We won't know until we try."

We placed the homemade bombs in spots we figured J. D. and his men would use as a rampart behind which to hide when they attacked. We placed one in the holding shed where we stabled the waiting pony, four or five in the limbs of large pines, and two in the log rack from which we cut our firewood.

After placing the bombs, I stashed spare cartridges in the barn in case one of us had to fort up there. With Darcy in the station and me in the barn, we could get them in a crossfire.

I kept glancing toward Daggett Pass, each time expecting to see J. D. Andrews and his owlhoots coming down the trail.

Mid-morning, three evenly spaced shots came from Kingsbury Grade. I replied with three of my own and minutes later, the westbound came in on schedule.

Mort Kenyon shook his head and sipped his steaming coffee when I asked about strangers. "Nope. Didn't see no one, but I did spot a campfire in a canyon up by the pass."

Darcy and me looked at each other. That was where we found the gold.

"Well, Gabe," the rider said, tossing Friday the cup and swinging back into the saddle. "You take care. See you in a couple of days."

* * *

Back in the station, Darcy poured some coffee. "What do you reckon J. D. is up to? I figured he'd be pounding on our door by now."

I stared in the direction of Daggett Pass. "I reckon he's planning on coming in tonight." I rose and peered out the window. "Of course, he might have spies out right now."

"Yep." Darcy nodded. "But knowing J. D., he won't. Him and those owlhoots are probably up there sleeping off a drunk."

We looked at each other.

His eyes danced with amusement. "You thinking what I'm thinking?"

"Reckon I am. If that's J. D. and his old boys up there, we might just narrow the odds down some."

Working fast, we built half a dozen more bombs, these with fuses. Then we loaded them in a bag along with a jar of coal oil to soak the fuses.

While we fashioned the explosives, Rock-in-Hand wrapped some grub and slipped it in my saddlebags. We took the Sharps and a Spencer, leaving the second Spencer with Joe Henry.

The cloud cover blocked out the sun, but I reckoned it was around noon when we pulled out on two spry mustangs. We kicked them into a running two-step, a mile-eating gait. Within half an hour, we reached the base of Kingsbury Grade and started our ascent.

Darcy kept his eyes forward. "You never did ask

where I hid the gold, Gabe." The words came out in frosty puffs.

I shrugged. "Nope. Don't reckon I did."

"Don't you want to know?"

"Not especially."

"What if something happens to me?"

"You always have Joe Henry. He can finish the job for you."

He laughed. In the crisp air, the sound was brittle. "You're a strange one, Gabe. Anybody else would be almighty anxious to know. Especially if you turn me in. Why, they would probably give you part of the gold as a reward."

I laughed with him. "I told you before, Darcy. I don't want nothing to do with it. If there's trouble coming like you suspect, it's going to pit brother against brother, American against American. The way I see it, the more I know about the gold, the more involved I am in something I don't want no part of. As far as turning you in . . . Well, you stole, and that ain't right. It's against the law, but it just seems that at the present, we got bigger problems."

He grew serious. "You can't run from it, Gabe."

"I'm not running. I'm just not helping."

Another two hours passed before we came in sight of Daggett Pass. We tied our ponies back among the rocks off trail. We studied the snow-covered trail, seeing no sentries. Slowly, we eased toward the rim of the canyon. The snow was tramped and scattered from horses coming and going.

We crouched in a small stand of young pines growing along the rim. Below, a fire blazed in front of a canvas fly that had been stretched between the wagon and two pines. Nearby, a dozen horses stood tied to a hitch rope. I looked for Sam, but he wasn't among the ponies.

Darcy nudged me with his elbow. "They look like they're warm and snug down there."

I grinned back. "Sure going to be a shame to disturb them. You think you can hit the fire from here?"

"Easy."

We dipped the cloth torches in the jar of coal oil.

"You put yours in the fire, and I'll drop one behind them." I fished a white phosphorus match from my pocket and struck it on the handle of my Colt.

We touched the fuses to the flames. A tiny flame erupted, sending a thin cloud of black smoke billowing into the crisp air. I nodded to Darcy. "Okay."

He hurled the glass bomb into the air. With flames trailing after, it arced through the air and dropped toward the fire. At the same time, I tossed mine at the rear of the overturned wagon. It fell several feet short.

His missile hit the canvas fly, smashing it to the ground. The jar rolled into the fire.

Startled voices broke the silence, followed moments later by a deafening explosion as the bomb blew the fire apart. In the next second, the bomb behind the wagon exploded.

Horses whinnied and reared, pawing at the hitch rope in an effort to break loose and escape the explosions.

Two more bombs followed, this time on either end of the wagon. Men scrambled from underneath the canvas fly and headed for the forest, bouncing off trees and each other as they blindly fled the bombing.

We each threw two more bombs after the fleeing men before hurrying back to our horses. Backtracking, we moved several hundred yards down the trail where it curved around a perpendicular bluff of granite.

I pulled up, laughing.

Darcy looked back up the trail. "If I know J. D., he's already lining his boys up to come after us."

"Then let him." Uncoiling my lariat, I cut it in two equal lengths, stretching the first neck high across the trail. A hundred yards down the trail, I stretched a second neck-breaker.

"Go on to the next bend. It almost double backs on itself. I'll meet you there. We'll toss a couple of more bombs on those that make it down to us."

"What are you going to do?"

I pulled the Sharps from the gunboot and inserted

a fresh paper charge and percussion cap. "I figure on giving them a reason to come after me. By the time I get back to you, we ought to be facing one or two less."

Chapter Fifteen

I reined up at the perpendicular bluff and waited. From where I sat on my pony, I had a clear view of two hundred yards of Kingsbury Grade. I figured I had time to get off half a dozen shots before I had to turn and run.

My Sharps rifle was a .52 caliber with a double-set trigger, and a Creedmore rear sight on a 28-inch octagonal barrel. That rifle was so accurate, I could knock the heart out of the Ace of Hearts at six hundred yards.

Naturally, such a feat was impossible offhand and astride a pony, but I could get close enough to those jaspers to dust the snow off their ten-gallon hats.

An hour passed. I was beginning to wonder if they'd gone back to Carson City.

They hadn't. Suddenly, dark figures appeared against the snow in the distance. I narrowed my eyes, trying to make out the figures.

They grew closer. I pulled the Sharps into my shoulder and aimed over their heads. I touched the hair trigger.

A deafening explosion broke the frigid silence and a burst of orange leaped from the muzzle. Its echo rolled through the canyons and down into Carson Valley. Quickly, I broke open the rifle, inserted another cartridge, and fitted another percussion cap on the nipple.

When I looked up, the shadows were milling about. I touched off another shot, this one into the ground in front of them. Horses whinnied in fright. Startled voices screamed out in fear.

Abruptly, bursts of orange appeared in the trail, followed in the next instant by the echo of gunfire. They were shooting back.

A faint voice drifted down the trail. "Rush him, boys, rush him!"

I jerked the Sharps to my shoulder, this time lining up on one of the orange bursts. I fired. The booming of the Sharps smothered the faint pops of their guns. A sudden burst of cursing told me I'd hit my target.

My pony milled about nervously. "Easy, boy, easy," I whispered, reloading once again. I held the reins in one hand and kept my knees tight on his ribs in an effort to steady the fidgeting animal.

I waited until they drew closer, then fired again. The group scattered, and I wheeled about, digging my heels into the mustang's flank. We raced down the trail.

Behind, a chorus of shouts arose. They thought they had me running scared.

Around the next bend, I leaned forward, lying on the mustang's neck as we sped under the first neck-breaker. Moments later, I swept past the second and slowed for the switchback in the trail.

Darcy called out, and I cut into the thicket of pine and fir. I reined up beside him. He grinned. "What happened? I heard shooting."

"I was just keeping them busy. I—" A scream cut off my explanation. "Someone got the rope," I whispered, chuckling.

Another scream echoed down the trail.

"And the second." Darcy laughed.

I slid the Sharps in the boot and pulled out my Colt. "They'll be here any time. You ready?"

He patted the butt of the Spencer. "Ready."

I peered through the thicket of willow and pines at the trail, wondering how many were left. We'd counted a dozen ponies at the fire. I figured I knocked one out of the saddle with the Sharps, and if we were lucky, we put two more out of the fight with the neck-breakers.

Minutes passed. Darcy looked around at me. "Where are they?"

I shrugged. "Maybe they had enough."

He snorted. "Not J. D. He'll do whatever it takes to get that gold. I know him."

Shadows began filling the forest.

Now I was puzzled. I was beginning to second-guess our plan. But what could have gone wrong? I wanted to believe Darcy was wrong, that J. D. had given up. But what if he hadn't quit? What if he'd decided to come at us from a different angle?

Maybe he was smart enough to figure out that he and his men were nothing more than sideshow targets if they stayed on the trail. I looked around, half expecting to see shadows creeping up on us from behind. The hair on the back of my neck tingled.

"Darcy."

He looked around at me.

"I think we best pull out."

"What do you mean? Those jaspers haven't gotten here yet."

I shivered. "I got a feeling they won't."

He looked at me, a frown wrinkling his forehead. He considered my reply for a few seconds. "You think they might have cut through somewhere, that they're between us and the way station?"

"I don't know, but just to look after our own skins, it's something we'd best consider." I shivered again, coming to grips with the chilling thought that J. D. and his men could be lying in ambush ahead.

"Well, then we best get out of here. You know this country good enough to take us through the forest back to the way station?"

By now, thicker shadows were filtering through the forest of pine and fir. Even with the darkness, we had hardly any chance of slipping past J. D. and his men unless we swung well off the trail, and that we couldn't do until we hit the bottom of the grade. "Once we reach the end of the grade, we can take to the forest." I shook my head. "Just hope he isn't waiting for us around the next bend."

"How far to the end?"

"Two, maybe three miles."

We eased from the thicket. I scanned the trail ahead, searching the tree line for any feature that didn't belong. Other than animal sign, the only tracks in the undisturbed snow along Kingsbury Grade were those Darcy and I made earlier.

Slowly, we made our way down the grade, expecting a barrage of lead plums at each step. But as each step passed, I breathed easier until we rounded the bend near the cave in which we had first hidden the wagon of gold.

I spotted a flash of fire from the forest ahead. From the corner of my mouth, I whispered, "Don't look around. Just follow me. Don't get spooky." I angled off the trail to the cave.

Darcy whispered, "What is it?"

I pointed to the cave for the benefit of those watching us. "Down below about a quarter-mile. Somebody's waiting for us. I spotted a match flame."

"J. D.?"

"I'd bet on it. Just act natural."

Dismounting, I led my mustang into the cave. Darcy followed. Once inside, I hurried to the pile of ashes that had once been our fire and kicked the blackened coals until I turned up some shards of lighter pine. Lighting them, I gave Darcy one. "Let's go."

I paid no attention to a portion of the cave wall that had collapsed near the fire.

A grin split the seriousness on his face. His eyes turned to the rear of the cave. "You're going to take us down the slope, huh?"

We headed down the long tunnel. I noticed tracks, but attributed them to the sign we had left a few days earlier.

After thirty minutes, Darcy chuckled. "How long do you figure they're going to wait on us?"

"Can't rightly say. I figure after a couple of hours, they'll grow plumb curious why there's no fire and send someone to see what's taking place."

It was still dark when we reached the mouth of the cave opening over the steep slope leading down to the old Daggett Pass Road. There was a three-foot drop from the cave to the slope. "High enough to bust one of our horse's legs," said Darcy.

"I'd as soon wait for sunup. Last thing we need is a horse with a broken leg."

Darcy looked back into the darkness of the cave behind us. "What if they're following?"

I gulped, then forced a laugh. "Then it could get mighty exciting around here."

He chuckled.

Sometime later, a false dawn crept across the forest.

I looked at Darcy. "Reckon it's time."

He nodded. "I reckon."

"Then let's do it gentle as we can."

Holding the reins of my mustang, I stepped down to the slope. Firmly, I pulled on the reins, holding the pony's head down. I didn't want him to jump, which would have surely broken something. With his head held down, he awkwardly slid his hooves down the side of the ledge to the slope. For a moment, he stood almost on his head until I eased him forward so his hind legs could slide down.

We did the same with Darcy's pony and gingerly led them down the jagged granite and sand slope to the road below, a slow, dangerous journey consuming over an hour.

The old Daggett Pass Road was overgrown and filled with snow, but it provided a direction for us back to the way station. I pointed along the road. "The way station is about three miles thataway."

"This trail leads to the station?"

"Yep."

The snow was not quite knee deep on our mustangs, so they were able to move easily. The morning sky was clear. The sun was hot. On the main trail, snow would begin to melt, but back in the forest among the shadows where we were, it remained crisp and solid, so solid the crust cracked and popped as we passed.

"Where are we now? Any idea?"

I glanced at the sun. "I figure we'll hit the main trail just below the base of Kingsbury Grade."

Darcy grunted. "Sounds like a good spot for J. D. and his boys to set up another ambush."

"Unless he doesn't have enough lard to fill the bucket, he would."

Laughing, Darcy replied, "J. D. was never one to use his brains."

"Well, then. Maybe he won't. Maybe we can slip in without trouble. But I don't think we need to use the main trail. Smart thing for us is to cut off this trail and angle through the woods to the station. I ain't the best tracker you ever seen, but I can keep a sense of direction."

Mid-morning, we cut off the old trail and wound our way through the towering ponderosa pine and white fir. Mountain chickadees darted about, tiny balls of white and black, settling in the tops of willows and fir. I kept glancing to my left, in the direction of the main trail.

I stiffened. In the distance, several hawks, both red-tailed and goshawk, circled and swirled, then vanished into the forest.

I had discovered early on that in a forest an hombre could get no idea of his surroundings if he just looked around at eye level. All he could see was a wall of tree trunks, but if he looked up, he could see gaps in the treetops in the distance, indicating a clearing, or what I was searching for, the main trail.

Abruptly, I reined up, still watching the birds.

Darcy pulled up beside me. "What is it?"

I pointed to our left. "Over there. See the gap in the treetops?"

"No. I don't—Yeah. Yeah, now I see. Maybe half a mile or so."

"See how the gap runs from left to right? That's the main trail. We'll leave our ponies here and ease over on foot. See what we can see."

He hesitated. "Why on foot? Why not just ride over?"

"Something spooked the hawks. I don't reckon they all spotted prey at the same time. I got me the feeling it was J. D. If we're lucky, we might just catch him and his boys napping."

Chapter Sixteen

Overhead, the clouds began to break.

The main trail was a bog of mud and snow, much too churned to be the result of two Express riders daily. J. D. and his boys had already passed.

"What do you think?" Darcy looked up and down the trail.

I studied the trail. A sense of urgency raised the hair on the back of my neck. "If I'm right, I think we'd better get on to the station. It'll take too long to go back for the horses."

He looked around at me, frowning. When he saw the concern on my face, he nodded toward the station. "You think J. D. is already there?"

I had already started west along the trail in a trot. "If he isn't, he soon will be."

Darcy hurried to catch up with me.

Within minutes, sweat rolled down my face. I loosened my coat. Ahead, the granite ridge rose from the snow. The station was just beyond.

Abruptly, gunfire erupted, the short popping sound of handguns punctuated by the boom of a Spencer. I motioned to the ridge with my Colt. "We got a half mile to go. I'll circle around to the barn. You find a spot to fort up near the station. Wait until I signal—two shots, a two-count pause, then two more. That's when we'll open up. I'll try to keep you covered until you reach the cabin."

Gasping for breath, Darcy nodded.

I swung deeper into the woods, heading for the winding creek that curved behind the barn. The deeper pockets of snow slowed me. I kept my eyes moving, searching the forest around me for sign of any of J. D.'s boys. The gunfire remained back to my left, sporadic now.

When I reached the creek, I turned west, following its tortuous course. As I drew closer to the way station, I dropped down into the creek, putting the creek bank between me and those owlhoots attacking the station.

By now, the sun had passed mid-sky and began dropping behind the pines. A fresh wind blew in from the north. I glanced up. No clouds, fresh wind. A frigid night. A fresh gust blew across my face. I looked at the sky again, spotting some thin mares' tails high against the pale blue sky. Maybe more than frigid. That gave me another idea.

Finally, I reached the dead embers of the Paiute campfire on the creek bank. The barn, its roof covered with layers of snow, sat in the timber fifty feet away. From time to time, gunshots emanated from the barn, causing the ponies inside to whinny and neigh. I could hear hooves nervously pounding against the board and batten side of the barn.

My first job was to take care of those jaspers inside. Two at least, maybe a third.

Having been out in the sun, I knew that when I stepped into the darkened barn, I'd almost be blind for several seconds, an easy potshot for anyone with such a mind.

Gun in hand, I eased toward the corrals in a crouch, peering between the rails through the open door at the milling ponies in the dark stalls inside. At the end of the barn was an open window through which we tossed hay to the horses in the corral.

I pressed up against a corral post, breathing hard, expecting the impact of a 200-grain slug at any moment. Luckily for me, the hombres inside were watching the station, not the corral.

I started to make a break for the barn, but a movement at the end of the building stopped me. I waited, watching for the movement again. Then I spotted it. One of the gunmen was in the window at the end of the barn.

Waiting until he fired and ducked, I slipped through the rails, dropped to my knees, and hurriedly crawled into the first stall and fell to my stomach on the hay. I listened intently, trying to pick apart the sound of the shadows beyond.

I guessed from the gunshots that the second gunman was at the front door. Moving slowly, I eased along the wall of an empty stall. The stalls had no gates, only a tie rope across the stall entrance to keep the horses inside.

Pressing my face into the hay on the ground, I peered around the corner of the entrance, squinting into the shadows. Silhouetted against the door at the end of the hay-covered corridor, a thickset cowpoke knelt and fired at the station.

I couldn't rush him. There was too much open space between us. He'd spot me before I was halfway across the barn floor.

Then I spotted the rope hanging from a pulley fastened to the rafters. On occasion, the Holston Stage Company stored goods in the loft. Maybe I could find another use for the rope and pulley.

Staying on the balls of my feet, I darted across the corridor and shinnied up the ladder to the loft.

I fashioned a loop in the rope. My plan was simple. I'd drop the rope over his arms, jump from the loft, and pull him off the ground.

What I didn't consider was that I was just a skinny drink of water. Later, I realized just what a dumb move it was, but I guess the old saw about God looking after fools and children had more truth to it than I figured.

Well, the first step went smoothly. I dropped the loop over his arms, and in those first few seconds when he was too startled to react, I jumped from the loft, holding tight to my end of the rope.

He shot off the ground a few feet, but his weight quickly slowed his ascent, and there we were, almost eye-to-eye, glaring at each other.

"Why, you—" he growled, trying to bring his handgun up.

I didn't waste time on words. I kicked him in the face with the heel of my boot, and that's when the rafter snapped from our struggles.

There was a loud crack, a sharp snap, a horrified scream, and we fell, pulling half the roof down and, to my good fortune, right on top of the second gunmen.

The one with the rope around his arms tried to sit up, but I whopped him across the head with my handgun. He collapsed.

The gunfire ceased because of the commotion. J. D. Andrews called across the clearing, "Hank! You okay?"

I yelled back. "No, J. D. He ain't okay." And I emptied my handgun in the direction of his voice. I reloaded and gave Darcy the signal.

From his hiding spot, Darcy broke for the cabin,

firing his handgun as he sprinted across the clearing, and for the next few minutes, lead plums flew back and forth like a swarm of bees chasing after a drunk queen.

The firing faded away somewhat, and that's when I decided to burn the barn despite the supply of Spencer cartridges I'd tucked away in one corner. If the weather turned as bad as I expected, J. D. and his boys would be more concerned about freezing than the gold.

I eyed the two unconscious owlhoots. I couldn't leave them to burn, so I dragged them out the back door and deposited them several yards away in the snow. I yanked off their boots and tossed the footwear into the creek.

Back in the barn, I filled my pockets with cartridges, then I swung open the barn door, touched a match to the dry hay, and turned the mustangs loose.

Frightened by the smell of smoke and the crackling of flames, the ponies bolted. Grabbing a handful of mane, I swung onto a little bay and guided her toward the station. As we swept past, I leaped from her back.

I hit on my feet and stumbled forward, slamming my head into one of the posts supporting the porch. Something stung my face, and I bounced back to the ground on my rump. Lurching forward, I blindly crawled the last half-dozen feet to the door and banged on it. I heard slugs thudding into the walls around me.

The door swung open, and I lunged inside.

Darcy slammed the heavy slab door as a spray of slugs tore into it.

Rock-in-Hand knelt by me, touching a damp rag to my face to wash away the blood. I winced as she pulled splinters from my face. Later, I discovered that a slug had torn into the post just as I bounced off, spraying my cheekbone with splinters. If I hadn't bounced off, I would have been walking around with no head.

I nodded slowly as she patiently worked on me. "The children?"

"Good," she mumbled.

I looked up into her face. Her jaw was set, her eyes steely. My first thought was that she was angry. But over what?

Before I could consider her mood any longer, another burst of gunfire raked the station.

Darcy returned the fire. At the end of the room, Joe Henry emptied his Colt while Friday reloaded the Spencer. I sure wished for the other Spencer and the Sharps, but they were back on the horses almost a mile away.

Struggling to my feet, I peered out through one of the gun ports. To my chagrin, none of J. D.'s boys were near the bombs we had planted. I shook my head. *Would you believe it,* I told myself, touching off a shot at a pine behind which an owlhoot was hiding.

Throughout the afternoon, we kept up a steady fire.

"At least we have plenty ammunition," Darcy muttered.

By now, the sun had fallen below the horizon, painting the western sky a soft pink and orange. Random flashes of orange exploded in the growing darkness, some in the proximity of the bombs, but it was too dark for us to hit them. We'd have to wait until morning.

Abruptly, three shots broke the silence.

Darcy peered out the gun port. "I don't see anyone out there. Wonder what's going on?"

"It's the Express rider signal. If I fire three shots, he'll come in."

"What if you don't?"

"He'll go around." I leaned back against the wall, wondering what the night would bring.

Darcy glanced at me. Without leaving his window, he asked, "Why'd you burn the barn? You ain't got no horses for the Express riders now."

My eyes found those of Rock-in-Hand, which were fixed on me. Without taking my eyes from hers, I replied, "Tonight's going to be bad cold. Cold enough to freeze the tail off the tiger. Without the barn, J. D. and his boys got no shelter save what they can rig."

Joe Henry spoke up. "What if they try to burn us out?"

"Let 'em try. These old logs take a while to get started. We keep a close eye on them. If we see they're going to give it a try, we'll go out after them."

A soft voice interrupted me. "Gabe?"

It was Friday. He held up a cup of coffee to me. "I put whiskey in it for you."

I scrubbed my fingers in his hair. "Thanks, boy. I can use it."

The frown had disappeared from Rock-in-Hand's face. "I bring you something to eat."

I nodded. "Thanks."

Chapter Seventeen

Far back in the forest beyond the clearing, a fire blazed.

"Looks like they decided to hole up for the night," Joe Henry said, peering out the gun port.

"Well, now, Joe, don't get too confident," drawled Darcy. "I got a feeling they're going to make one or two tries tonight."

I grunted. "Hope you're wrong. If it was me out there, I'd build me a nice, warm snow house and curl up inside my tarp."

"Hey, what happened to the fire out there?" Joe's voice broke.

Quickly, I rose and peered into the night. From time to time, I caught a glimpse of fire. "Appears to me, they're rigging a tent to hold the fire's heat."

"Yep." Darcy looked round at our fire. "But I reckon I'd much prefer this one we got."

While we talked, Rock-in-Hand fed the children and made them ready for bed. I couldn't help noticing just how those little youngsters did everything she said. I hated it that she'd lost her own child. She was a fine mother. I wondered about her husband. What kind of man he had been? And to my surprise, I felt a touch of jealousy.

Later, as the fire burned low, I peered out the rear gun port and whispered to Darcy, "We need those two rifles we left with our ponies. I'm going for them. Probably take a couple hours. Three knocks on the back door, throw it open."

He studied me a moment, the low flames dancing in the fireplace sprinkling our faces with shadows of orange. "Take care."

I nodded, pulled on my mackinaw, and tugged my hat down over my ears. Rock-in-Hand laid her hand on my arm. "Gabe look close."

"Closer than you think," I said, grinning at her. I shucked my handgun, and slipped out the back door.

When I heard the locking bar drop in place inside, I suddenly felt I was all alone in the world.

I stood in the shadows of the station for several minutes, studying the forest before me. I examined each shadow, noting how it moved with the wind. Then about thirty yards out, I spotted a shadow moving even when the wind laid. Whatever it was, I told myself, it was not a stunted pine or fir.

I crept along the back of the station until I had the thick bole of a ponderosa pine between me and the shadow.

Silently, I ghosted across the snow and pressed up against the scaly bark of the pine. I peered around the trunk, found the shadow, then darted to another pine, trying to work around to the side.

If it was a sentry, I wanted to slip past without disturbing him. If I coldcocked him, he might awaken before I returned and have half a dozen of J. D.'s cronies waiting for me.

I slipped to another tree, then another, each time expecting the impact of a slug, but within minutes, I was a hundred yards from the station. I breathed easier as I pushed through the snow to the horses.

They whinnied when they spotted me. I decided to move them closer and soon I found a thicket of willow, small fir, and antelope brush that would break the wind. I shivered as I tied them. The night was growing colder.

I grabbed the Sharps and Spencer and headed back.

When I was within a hundred yards or so of the sentry, I grew more cautious. I wanted to spot him first. I didn't need any shooting for that would draw unwanted attention. That meant I had to get close enough to knock him out.

Then I spotted him. The shadows cast by the moving trees and limbs distorted my perception. On occasion, I thought he was looking straight at me, on others, watching the station.

I crept forward.

Suddenly, a guttural voice broke the silence. "All right, hombre. Just hold it right there."

I froze.

A muzzle jabbed me in the side as the shadow I'd been watching leaped to his feet. He hurried to me.

"What you got there?" the approaching sentry asked.

"Don't rightly know. He's out here prowling around. Can't be one of them inside. You said none of them came out."

I seized the moment. "Sorry to disturb you, gents. I got lost. Been wandering all night. Sure be obliged if you could see your way clear to put me up." I shivered. "Getting mighty cold out here."

The muzzle jerked back, and a hand spun me around. A familiar face leered at me. "Why, hello there, Gabe. Surprised to see you out here."

Even in the shadows, I made out the mocking face of J. D. Andrews!

He barked at the approaching sentry, "You blasted jughead. This is one of them. I thought you told me no one had come out."

The sentry stopped behind me. Before he could answer, a dark figure stepped from behind a pine and swung a club, smashing J. D. Andrews in the back of the skull. The lanky man groaned and folded to the snow.

I spun, swinging the rifles. The butt of the Spencer caught the sentry on the point of the jaw. He collapsed without a sound.

I looked around.

Rock-in-Hand!

"What are you—"

She rushed past me. "Inside. There are others out here."

We dashed for the cabin. She banged three times on the door. It swung open, and we lunged inside.

I leaned against the door, gasping for breath. Finally I turned to Rock-in-Hand who was staring at me, a cryptic smile on her face. "How did you know I was out there?"

Darcy snorted. "She's been out there waiting since just after you left." He grinned at me as if he were trying to tell me something, but I was too dense to understand.

"Huh?"

He shook his head. "Never mind."

I looked back at Rock-in-Hand, but she was tending the infant.

With a shrug, I laid the rifles on the table. Now we had some firepower. As soon as the sun rose, we'd have enough light so we could touch off the homemade bombs.

Maybe that would convince J. D. Andrews to reconsider the job he had cut out for himself.

Shedding my heavy coat, I poured some coffee and sat at the table, reloading the Sharps and checking the cartridge tube of the Spencer.

Next thing I knew, someone was shaking me awake. "Huh? What?" I blinked and looked around. The room had grown lighter. The sun was up. I shook my head. "I must've fallen asleep."

Joe sat across the table from me. "Yes, sir, and you was sawing logs like you planned to build a brand-new cabin."

Darcy leaned against the wall, his eye at the gun port. I rolled my shoulders in an effort to ease the stiffness in my neck. "Anything going on out there?"

He clicked his tongue. "Nothing. That worries me. I'd expected some surprise from J. D. by now."

I tossed my cold coffee in the back of the hearth and poured a fresh, hot cup. It warmed me going down. "Maybe he doesn't have any more surprises up his sleeve."

"Not likely. J. D. always has a surprise. I've seen him—Hold on. There's one making a run for the holding shed."

A grin came to my face as I peered out the gun port. The shed was small, just the size to hold a single mustang out of the weather while waiting for the express rider to come in.

We had set the homemade bomb on the ground by the corner post and covered it with snow and mud except for the one spot marking the handful of percussion caps.

"Think you can hit it?" I looked at Darcy.

"Nothing to it. Just watch."

He slid the barrel of the Spencer out the gun port, steadied it, and touched off a shot. The crack of the rifle split the crisp silence of the icy morning. Moments later, a reverberating explosion bounced off the walls of the way station.

When the smoke cleared, the shed had disappeared. A motionless figure lay sprawled in the snow. I chuckled. "Well, Darcy, I do believe you hit your target."

Shots rang out and splatted against the gun port. Darcy ducked and said, "Yep, and they don't seem none to happy about it."

I noticed Rock-in-Hand tilt her head and freeze. She seemed to be listening to something. I always had good ears, but I heard nothing. "What is it?"

She gestured toward Daggett Pass. "Men leave. Many horses."

I peered out a gun port, but I saw no movement at all. "I don't see a thing."

She nodded emphatically. "Many horses."

Darcy looked at me quizzically. "You think she's right?"

"I didn't hear a thing."

Still pointing to Daggett Pass, she added, "Some stay. Many ride away."

I eyed the front door curiously.

Darcy had the same idea. "One way to find out, Gabe."

We stood on either side of the door. I moved Rock-in-Hand and the children out of the way of fire, then nodded to Darcy. "Throw it open."

As soon as the door swung open, a barrage of gunshots erupted. Slugs slammed into the door and wall. I kicked the door shut immediately. "Well, one thing for sure," I said, going back to my gun port. "There's some still out there."

"Then where do you figure the others were going?"

I stared at him. "Beats me."

We found out that night.

Joe Henry's startled voice roused me from a restless sleep. "What are they doing now?"

Blinking the sleep from my eyes, I squinted into the starlit night. Across the clearing was the wagon that had tumbled down into the canyon. J. D. and his men had pulled it out and stacked it high with limbs and branches.

I felt Rock-in-Hand at my back. I moved slightly

so she could peer out the gun port with me. As we looked on, the night grew darker, and the starlight faded.

Moments later, a torch flared, casting a flickering light on the wagon. One of the cowpokes on horseback threw the torch on the pile of branches in the wagon.

"They're going to burn us out," Joe exclaimed.

"Not if I can help it," I muttered, sliding the barrel of the Sharps through the gun port. I put the sights in the middle of the horseman's chest and squeezed. The rifle boomed, and the rider somersaulted backward from his saddle.

Quickly, I reloaded and touched off two more shots, sending the riders scurrying for cover.

The fire in the wagon flickered, then grew brighter. I grimaced. The wagon and its load of fuel would create a fire of such intensity that it would consume even the thick walls of the waystation.

I glanced in the direction of the trapdoor leading to the tunnel. We couldn't take the children out. The weather was too frigid and chilling, especially without a fire. And without a fire, they'd never survive the night.

I wasn't born in the woods to be scared by an owl, but at the time, I was at a loss for a course of action. The best we could hope for was to do as much damage with our weapons as we could before we were forced to leave the station.

Darcy shouted, "Look! Look! Is that what I think it is? Snow?"

We could see the flakes between us and the blazing fire. They fell faster and heavier.

I pounded my fist against the wall in glee. "Snow, snow, snow," I muttered through clenched teeth. "That'll stop them."

"For tonight," Darcy replied.

"That's okay. Just let it keep snowing."

And it did. Within minutes, the fire in the wagon was out. I grinned at Rock-in-Hand. We'd made it through the night.

To celebrate, we brewed a fresh pot of six-shooter coffee. We remained at our posts while Friday passed the cups around.

"What about tomorrow?"

I looked at Darcy who was peering out the gun port. "Reckon we'll take that when it gets here."

He turned to me and shook his head. "Look. J. D. wants the gold. I'll tell him where it is. That'll satisfy him."

"No." I shook my head. "We're not quitting. The only thing I ever gave to someone who threatened me was a mouthful of knuckles. I'm too old to change."

Darcy started to argue, but I continued, "Besides, I think I know how you and I can get out there tonight and narrow the odds."

A frown knit his eyebrows. "Narrow the odds? How? They'll cut us down soon as we step outside."

"Suppose I told you I could get us out of here without anyone being wiser?"

Friday stared up at me, his forehead wrinkled in a frown.

Darcy laughed derisively. "I'd say you was some kind of magician."

My grin grew wider.

He eyed me curiously. "Are you some kind of magician?"

I shrugged and winked at Friday. "Could be."

Chapter Eighteen

The others overheard our conversation. Joe Henry stood at the gun port, eyeing us with interest. Rock-in-Hand moved a step toward us, her face reflecting her own curiosity.

"A tunnel."

He stared at me in disbelief. "A tunnel?"

I nodded to the far end of the room. "Under the bunk in the corner. It comes out back near the creek in a tumble of fallen pines. I figure we can slip out, do some damage, and sneak back in before they know what hit them."

A slow grin spread over his face. "I wouldn't mind getting a chance at J. D., but how? With no moon or stars out, we'll be stumbling in the dark."

I shrugged. "No. Once your eyes adjust, you can

163

pick out the difference between snow and trees. Besides, we'll have his fire to guide on."

Darcy mulled over my reply. "Just what do you have up your sleeve?"

I indicated the gun port to Joe Henry. "Keep a good eye, Joe. With the storm, I figure they'll hole up in their tent tonight."

He grinned. "You bet."

Sipping my coffee, I considered a course of action. "First, you know that as soon as the snow stops, they're going to send that wagon at us."

I looked at Rock-in-Hand. I saw her answer in the resolution in her eyes.

"Yeah," Darcy growled.

"Okay, then here's what I have in mind."

Far back among the pine and fir, flames cast eerie shadows on the thick boles of the trees. Earlier, I had considered taking potshots at the flames, but J. D. Andrews was too smart for me. By moving so far back in the forest, he utilized the trees as an ideal fortification. Even the Sharps' 475-grain slug powered by 50 grains of powder wouldn't penetrate such a defense.

After an hour of watching and waiting, I cleared my throat. "Reckon some are snoozing off now. We might as well get moving."

I glanced at the children. Phillip and Mary were sleeping peacefully by the fire. The infant lay awake, fascinated by her hands. Friday stood at my side. I laid my hand on his shoulder. "You help Joe and Rock-in-Hand, you hear?"

He nodded, his eyes reflecting his fear and trepidation.

"We'll be fine, boy. Just you do what I asked."

"I will, Gabe."

Frigid air smelling of coal oil billowed up from the dark hole when I threw open the trapdoor.

"What's that smell?" Joe Henry wrinkled his nose.

"Coal oil. Keeps the snakes out of the tunnel."

Darcy hesitated. "Snakes? What do you mean snakes?"

I slung the Sharps over my back, dropped down into the tunnel, and looked back up. "You know, Darcy. The kind that crawl on their bellies. They love ready-built tunnels like this to hibernate in. The coal oil keeps them out."

"You sure?"

I reached for the lantern. "No, but if there are any down here, they're so cold, they can't move. Why, you could probably dance one of those Southern hoedowns with one looped around your neck." I laughed.

He gave me a wry grin. "I suppose I'll let someone else give that a try."

I dropped to my knees and headed out. Darcy followed.

Minutes later, we crawled from the tunnel and paused in the middle of the jumble of fallen pines. Peering into the darkness, I whispered, "You know what to do, so let's do it. It's cold as a wagon tire out here. Just give me time to place the bombs."

He grunted. "Don't worry."

We split up. Darcy was to circle and come in on the camp from the west, me from the east. I had no idea how many owlhoots had stayed with J. D., but I figured if we put two or three down, the others might decide to take another look at J. D.'s plan.

I headed for the log rack, planning on retrieving the two bombs we had placed there. I didn't expect any sentries out, but I moved cautiously.

Suddenly, the snowflakes stopped striking my cheek. I looked up, exposing my face to the falling snow. There was none. Had the storm passed so quickly?

Overhead, a few clouds parted, and abruptly, a glittering patch of stars shone through, casting a bluish light on the snow.

I cursed our luck under my breath. An hour's worth of sunlight would melt the snow from the wagon.

After recovering the two bombs, I removed a third one from a forked willow branch. I crouched behind a pine on the edge of the clearing and studied the wagon nearby. There was no one around.

Rising into a crouch, I ghosted across the clearing

to the wagon. Just as I reached it, a shadow jumped from behind the wagon wheel with a startled gasp. "Hey! Who is that? Luke?"

I thought fast. "Yeah. Here. Hold this." I handed him a bomb, and then with my free hand, I shucked my sixgun and laid it across his forehead. He dropped like a pole-axed steer.

Quickly retrieving the bomb, I packed it and the other two among the thick-laced branches in the wagon bed. If the fire didn't set them off, maybe we could with the Spencers.

I glanced at the sprawled gunman, unslung the Sharps from my back, and headed for the owlhoots' camp. Overhead, the patch of stars grew larger as the clouds marched south.

I glanced back to my right, hoping Darcy didn't mistake me for one of J. D.'s boys. Through the trees ahead, I spotted their shelter, several tarps strung together in a three-sided windbreak with a canvas roof. The tent was a crude, but effective, protection against the weather.

Just before I reached the camp, I spotted a dark figure standing next to a pine. He had his back to me. I moved slower, pushing my feet through the snow instead of lifting and setting them down, a trick taught me by the Pawnee I had once lived with.

I eased closer, holding my breath.

He groaned, shrugged his shoulders, and shivered. Abruptly, he turned and stared at me in surprise.

Without hesitation, I jammed the butt of the Sharps in his belly.

He grunted sharply and doubled over.

I straightened him with the butt to the forehead. He collapsed without a sound.

Behind me, the unmistakable roar of a Spencer shattered the icy silence, followed by a pain-filled scream. I pulled my own rifle to my shoulder as one of the owlhoots ran from the tent, gun in hand. I put a slug in his leg. He screamed and spun as he tumbled to the ground.

Darcy fired again. I quickly reloaded. I was tempted to fire into the tent, but Darcy was on the far side. I might hit him, so I stepped behind a pine and waited.

In the meantime, the string of horses tied to the hitching rope was rearing and pawing the air in fright. The rope parted, and the horses disappeared into the night.

I grinned and touched off another shot into the air. Maybe we'd convinced some of them to ride on out once they caught their ponies. I gave a short whistle and headed back to the way station.

When I passed the wagon, I noticed the hombre I'd knocked down had disappeared.

Darcy was waiting for me at the entrance to the tunnel. He chuckled. "How many did you get?"

"Three. One won't be walking without a crutch.

The other two are going to have some mighty sore skulls."

"I got two."

"Looks like we made a dent in that bunch." I gestured to the tunnel. "Let's go."

We sat around the sawbuck table sipping six-shooter coffee and laughing about our little jaunt. Friday sat at my side. Joe Henry leaned against the wall beside his gun port. He peered out, then turned back to us. "How many were out there? Could you tell?"

"Nope," I replied, shaking my head.

"I counted nine horses," said Darcy.

"That means there's probably only four or five healthy enough to go on with the fight, huh?" I heard the hope in Joe Henry's voice.

Darcy grunted. "Probably."

I looked at Rock-in-Hand. "The kids are okay?"

"Yes. They do not cry. They are strong. Like the Washoe." There was a look of pride on her face.

Friday leaned against me. "I did not cry, Gabe. I did as you said. I am a warrior."

I hugged him to me. "Reckon you are, boy. I'm proud of you."

With the rising sun, my heart sank. The sky was clear as spring water. We peered through the gun ports, searching for any sign of J. D. or his men.

"Nothing," said Darcy, allowing a grin to play over his face.

"At least, so far," Joe Henry added.

"Another hour, we'll have visitors."

Both men looked at me.

Chapter Nineteen

I missed my prediction by thirty minutes. The first notice we got was a cowpoke on horseback streaking from behind the granite ridge carrying a blazing torch. Two more were right behind him, leaning low over their ponies.

They somehow made it through the screen of lead we threw at them. The first torch hit the stacked limbs and bounced to the ground, but the other two fell down inside the stacks and began burning.

Moments later, the riders made another pass.

This time, Joe Henry knocked one from his saddle, but the other two put their torches in the wagon.

The fire intensified.

All we could do was sit and watch hopelessly. That's when I spotted the two ropes tied to the wagon tongue and one to each rear corner of the wagon.

An old Indian trick, and a good one. Riders grabbed the ropes and while their compadres sprayed the building with lead, they got the wagon moving at a fast clip, and at the last minute, turned it loose and let it roll on its own momentum right into the way station.

"Okay, boys," I said, bringing my Sharps to my shoulder. "Let's us pepper that wagon with lead. I packed three of those homemade bombs in there. If the fire don't set 'em off, maybe we can."

As if my words were the signal, a barrage of lead slammed into the waystation, several smashing through the gun ports, forcing us to keep our heads down.

Hunkered down, I looked at Darcy. "It appears to me that all we did last night was make those old boys mad."

He grinned. "Appears likely."

I cocked my rifle. "Well, let's get in our share."

We jerked upright and blasted the wagon with lead.

From the far end of the room, Rock-in-Hand peered through a crack in one of the slab shutters. "The wagon is rolling."

I quickly reloaded. "Shoot fast, boys. It's time to post up or pull foot, and we ain't got no place to pull foot to."

We returned their murderous fire. I managed to get off several slugs directly into the inferno atop the wagon. The heavy Sharps's slug tore chunks from the wagon's splashboard and shattered burning limbs, but the wagon kept coming. I grimaced and fired again.

For a brief second, a flash of sunlight reflected from one of the glass bombs. Instantly, I squeezed off a shot. Just before the riders dropped their ropes and swung away, the wagon exploded, catching all four men and animals in its blast, hurtling them several yards through the air.

The explosion disintegrated the wagon.

Two jaspers rose from the willows at the edge of the forest and stared at the burning wagon. I knocked one down with a slug to the shoulder, and Darcy hit the other.

He looked at me and grabbed a handful of full cartridge tubes. "I'd say we been in here long enough."

We charged out the door. I zigzagged toward the wood rack, trying to outguess the slugs popping into the snow and mud at my feet. I promised myself right then if I lived through this, I'd never get myself in this kind of fix again.

I leaped over the top of the log rack, tumbling to the ground on the far side. Instantly, I jumped to my feet and jammed the Sharps into my shoulder. Two cowpokes were heading for me.

When they spotted me, they dodged, but I caught the first one in the chest. I dropped the Sharps and shucked my Colt. I hit the second one in the rear just as he ducked behind a large ponderosa. He spun out on the other side and sprawled to the ground, clutching the back of his trousers.

I don't know where Darcy went, for I had been a mite too busy to worry about him. I jerked around. Darcy stood in the middle of the clearing facing away from me. Standing between Darcy and me was a cowpoke in a green-and-black mackinaw drawing down on the Reb.

"Darcy!"

The cowpoke spun and fired. I beat him to the trigger. His slug tore into a log at my feet, but I hit him hard. He stiffened in surprise, then placed his hand to his chest. He pulled it away and stared at the blood. He looked back at me in disbelief, and then his legs folded under him.

A familiar voice sounded behind me. "Hello, Gabe." It was J. D. Andrews. I heard him cock the hammer. He had me cold. "Let's just see how fast you are."

At that moment, Rock-in-Hand's voice cut through the cold air. "No."

J. D. hesitated, momentarily distracted, but that's all I needed. I dropped into a crouch and spun, pumping off shot after shot as I came around.

Something hit me in the shoulder, knocking me

backward, then in the thigh, slamming my leg from under me and driving me to my knees, and then a blow cracked my head, but I kept firing until the trigger fell on an empty chamber.

My nostrils stung from the acrid smell from the haze of gunsmoke clouding the air. As it cleared, I saw J. D. Andrews sprawled on the ground, a gaping hole in his throat and two over his heart.

Darcy hurried up to me, his face tight with alarm. "Gabe! You hurt bad?"

I looked around at him and tried to grin. "I—I don't think so, but you look like you're wobbling something fierce." The next thing I saw was blackness.

The first thoughts that came to me was just how wonderfully sinful was the smell of fried steak, red-eye gravy, sourdough biscuits, and hot coffee. If this were heaven, I wouldn't complain. I opened my eyes and stared at the rafters over my head.

I turned my head. The shutters were open, and a bright sun laid out rectangular blocks of yellow on the puncheon floor.

Rock-in-Hand was kneeling at the hearth, her back to me.

A tiny voice spoke at my ear. "Hello."

I looked around. Mary smiled down at me. Phillip just frowned. "You're alive," the small girl announced.

"I hope so." I tried to grin, but my head exploded. I closed my eyes and prayed for the pain to subside. Slowly, ever so slowly, it did.

I heard the running of footsteps and the muffled voices of the children. When I opened my eyes, Rock-in-Hand was looking down at me, tears in her eyes. "You are hungry?"

Somehow, tears in her eyes and her question if I was hungry didn't fit together. I was too woozy to try to figure it out, but not so out of sorts not to be hungry. In fact, I was starving. I nodded slowly. "Yes. I'm hungry."

Friday entered and when he saw I was awake, rushed to me. Gleefully, he cried out, "Gabe!" He started to jump on me, but a warning from Rock-in-Hand stopped him. He grinned sheepishly. "You okay?"

"I think so." I struggled to sit up. Friday and Rock-in-Hand helped me get comfortable, and then she heaped me a plateful of grub.

While she fed me, she explained that I had been unconscious for five days. "Darcy and Joe bury men," she said. "They find ponies for riders. Friday get ponies ready. He do good work."

I smiled gratefully, and proudly, at the boy. "He's a good boy."

Sipping the coffee, I realized I wasn't as hungry as I thought. "I'll eat more later," I said, leaning back and closing my eyes. "Where's Darcy now?"

"He and the boy go. They take men's horses. Darcy say you find more ponies in cave."

I slipped back into a deep, healing sleep.

The next morning, I managed to get to my feet. My leg was stiff as a post. Luckily, the slug just took a chunk from my thigh.

I was weak as pond water. The ponies could wait. Another day or so would make no difference. That evening, Johnny Fry came through on the eastbound.

"See you're going to live, huh?" He sipped his coffee and whiskey.

"Looks like it, Johnny."

"By the way. Remember that stink about the stolen Yankee gold?" I nodded, and he continued, "Well, sir. Talk about just desserts. Seems like that gold was Southern gold mined by Southern boys in the California goldfields. A bunch of Union sympathizers stole it, and then some Southern boys stole it back." He laughed. "Ain't that a hoot?"

A weight lifted from my shoulders. I just shook my head. "Seems like to me, everyone is trying to take from someone else, don't it?" And right then, I was glad I never had the chance to turn Darcy over to the law.

He swung into the saddle. "It sure do, Gabe. It sure do. Oh, yeah, got a letter for you from Sacramento—the main office." He handed me a sealed envelope.

"Thanks." I took it, and he headed out with a holler and hoot.

I stared at the envelope for several seconds before going inside and pouring a cup of coffee. I sat at the table and opened the envelope. Friday and Rock-in-Hand sat beside me.

The words in the letter hit me in the pit of the stomach. Suddenly, I was exhausted.

Rock-in-Hand read the weariness on my face and realized it came from the letter. "Something is wrong?"

Slowly, I nodded. Suddenly, I had a mountain to climb. "Reckon you could say that. I wrote a letter to the banker in Sacramento about the children. Trying to find their family."

As one, we looked at Mary and Phillip who were sitting beside the infant entertaining her.

"Seems like the kids got no family. The story the banker told the main office was that the Wagners sold everything after her mother died. No relatives, so they came out here to start over."

"What happen to children now?" Rock-in-Hand's voice trembled. I saw dread in her eyes.

"Well, they got a couple of thousand in the bank." I laughed bitterly. "I suppose I'll send them on to Sacramento. I reckon a lot families would take them in for that kind of money."

She just stared at me, a cryptic, accusing look in her eyes.

I knew exactly what she was thinking. I shook my head. "Now, I can't keep them. I got a cattle drive in another month or so. And then a ranch in Wyoming."

For several moments, she eyed me. "That not what you say before."

As much as I hated to admit it, she was right. I had popped off about keeping the children. But that was just talk. Half joking. At least, that's what I said in an effort to convince myself that I owed nothing to the children. Once they were gone, Rock-in-Hand would leave, and I'd head for South Texas with Friday. But then, to my surprise, I realized I didn't want Rock-in-Hand to leave.

My own life had been hard as dried rawhide. No child should have to face what I did. I studied the children. When they grew up, they'd soon enough find life was tough. They didn't need it any tougher than necessary until then.

I saw tears glitter in Rock-in-Hand's dark eyes.

I was whipped.

Finally, I shrugged. "Will you stay and help me with them?"

Her face beamed with delight. Her eyes danced. She nodded. "Yes, Gabe. I stay."

I looked around the waystation with a touch of resignation. "I don't know how long we'll be here, but I reckon I can always find another job once this one plays out."

We were both grinning now. An unspoken understanding passed between us, one as natural and honest as you could want. Friday looked at us, puzzled, unable to understand what we were talking about.

I slept better that night than I had in years despite the fact that I'd put a lifelong dream on hold for the children. And later I realized that was exactly why I had slept so well.

Chapter Twenty

Next morning, Friday and me rode up to the cave to round up the ponies and take them back to the station. I figured Darcy must have run across them in the forest. They certainly weren't in the cave when him and me passed through the last time although I did remember horse tracks in the sand.

The ponies were tied to a hitching rope, six of them. One end of the hitching rope was knotted around some saddlebags lying beside the dead ashes of the fire. And then I noticed that a portion of the wall had fallen.

Friday ran to the saddlebags. "I get bags, Gabe."

He yanked on the bags and almost yanked himself down. He looked up at me, puzzled.

"What the Sam Hill," I muttered, reaching for the

saddlebags. They were heavy. Frowning, I opened them.

A grin as wide as the Tahoe Valley split my face. I shook my head and looked to the south toward Louisiana and Texas. "Well now, Darcy. You can be a surprising man too."

In the saddlebags were four bags of gold. Forty pounds. Over twenty thousand dollars. More than enough for my Wyoming ranch and a herd of prime beef.

After all, I told myself, grinning at Friday, with four growing youngsters and wife, a man needed a heap of beef to put on the table.